GW00391165

This Page Was Left Blank Accidentally

Life Is What It Is. Or Was. Nothing Is Known. No Questions Can Be Answered. Question Everything. Question Yourself. Fear Is Your Only Friend.

10/8
£1.50

Arty Grape & The Ramblings Of A Madman

Copyright © 2019 Darius Z Sutherland
All rights reserved.
ISBN-13: 9781699347614

Cover by Jel - Dusted Design Brighton
Editor : Kristina Howell

I'd like to thank my lovely partner Naomi for letting me go to the pub to write this, for being a wonderful and forgiving person and always being there for me.

Important: If you find this book somewhere and you've finished reading it or don't want to read it, please leave it somewhere for somebody else to find. Maybe not when it's raining, preferably a warm and dry place. If you have one of those little sealable bags, you know the ones with a ziplock you can put in the fridge, that would be perfect. If not I find leaving it on a bus, train or a park bench is perfect. Failing that just hand it to a friend, you don't even have to like them that much.

Yours Gratefully, Darius Z. Sutherland.

The Next Day

She woke up the next day. It felt like it usually did, but it wasn't. There was something different but she didn't know what it was or where that feeling had come from. She was experiencing disturbing thoughts and uncomfortable feelings at regular intervals.

It was a school day and she did what she usually did at that time in the morning, which was limiting the chaos that was about to occur. She dragged her limbs out of the bed; it was her turn today to get the children ready for the day ahead. She put on her slippers and her dressing gown, and cleaned her teeth. As she walked out of the room she glimpsed at her husband lying in bed. He was dead to the world, exhausted by everything that had come before. She made her way up the stairs. She sleepwalked through every task and every conversation. Her children were awake and waiting for her, they sat on the sofa, they were dressed and they were ready for their breakfast. 'Good morning you two,' she said. 'What would you like to eat today?' They gave their answers without looking at her, it meant she could fully enjoy her autopilot mode. She prepared the breakfast feast, she tried to ensure it was something different and healthy each day. 'Come, sit down you two, eat your breakfast.' The children sat and they ate and then they brushed their teeth and got ready for the school day, and waited for the time to arrive when they needed to leave.

This is where things became very different to every other day that had ever passed. The clock in the town chimed, it had never chimed and on any other that that would have seemed strange, but today it didn't. The children put on their backpacks and were ushered out the front door. Normally she would wave them goodbye and give them a motherly kiss, but today was a different day. She opened the door and there stood a slender man (not the slender man you are thinking about, but slender nonetheless). The slender man had been waiting for the children to be delivered to him. He may have always been there but only now had he decided to be seen. Like the Devil and Death, waiting for you to make one simple mistake. It was impossible to describe his face. It was like watching a television that had no reception – in the good old days that is. His face appeared faceless to her, it was like the facelessness of the future; none of his features could be predicted. He wore a bowler hat that covered a bald head. There is no escaping the slender man in the town of Eden, when he comes for your children, you have no choice but to obey his orders. She was in a trance, she had become hypnotised by his face yet she was aware of everything that was happening. She glanced over the slender man's shoulder to discover the same thing happening elsewhere, it was like she was watching herself. At all the other houses stood another slender man, he was right in front of her and all around her at the same time. He was collecting all the other children from all the other houses. She gave her children to him without any hesitation, it was like she was glad to be rid of them, and her chance had come. Nobody knew who the slender man was but everyone seemed happy to see him, everyone was happy to deliver their children to him.

(It was seven years before all the children were returned,

and when they returned it was like they had never left, but they had been changed forever. All the children travelled to a strange place that they were all required to visit – and then they would come back again.)

Welcome to the town of Eden. Everything is normal in the town of Eden but everything is strange too, you'll see. We'll get to the town of Eden later but the first question we need ask ourselves is: Are the people in the town of Eden good people or bad people and am I thinking of the town of Eden at exactly the same time as you?

A Town Called Eden

Over the rolling hills and through a lush green forest lies a town called Eden. If you were to drive towards the rising sun until you could drive no further you would find a town that has been hidden away since time began. You'd more than likely get lost first, because who in their right mind drives towards the rising sun? (Most people would use a map). After the arduous journey you would realise it was worth it in the end, despite what other people may have said about it. Upon arrival through the mountains you would feel elated, you would smell the wonderful rose gardens from a great distance and you would smile at the scent of freshly baked bread lingering in the morning air. The sound of children giggling in the playgrounds would fill you with joy and you would have been welcomed with open arms as you walked through the rusty gates of heaven.

The people in Eden walk hand in hand, gazing at each other with loving smiles. They are kind with their words and warm with their embraces. Nothing bad happens in Eden. Does that sound wonderful? Unfortunately for you it's all lies, but only some if it. There *are* beautiful rose gardens and there *is* the sweet smell of freshly baked bread in the air, but you will struggle to hear the sound of any child laughing. Why, I hear you ask? The truth can only be discovered in the pages of this book and you will discover it, but not just yet. The discovery happens on the thirtyoneth page. Skip ahead right now and you will find that I have told you more lies. I am unsure of how many more lies I will tell you, you will just have to trust that I am telling you The Truth.

This story isn't about the town called Eden – or not entirely, at least – this is a story about a little girl called Arty Grape and her brother Mr Fox. Have patience my friend, we do get to them and all their shenanigans very soon. They are sleeping right now, resting before everything begins. But as you know, first things are first.

The town of Eden is indeed beautiful, if you were looking at it with a different kind of eyes. It was beautiful for the strangest of reasons that cannot be explained fully in this book, and I'm not sure you would fully understand them either, even when written down. I have often been asked what is the strangest thing about Eden? I would have to say it is the fact that no child could be found there. The children had disappeared long ago and nobody seemed to care. The people in the town of Eden didn't flinch at this strange occurrence because it wasn't strange to them. It was as normal as wearing sparkly red shoes to bed.

The town of Eden is isolated from the rest of the world and it only existed to some who knew how to get there, and only if they desired to get there. Only a small population of people had found the town of Eden and they didn't aspire to be anything else other than who they were. They had gathered, they had stayed, and they had populated the town. Aaaaaah, the beautiful town of Eden, it was surrounded by the tallest of mountains and a river would run through it for ten thousand more years. You could walk its entire length, resting at glorious waterfalls on your travels – you would have so much fun along the way. You will need to put your wellies on because you are sure to get wet. Just when you think your legs can't carry you any further you'll find yourself in the quaintest of spots. You will marvel at the sweet shops, cake shops, parks, playgrounds and ponds. If you should ever find Eden in your mind, the people are the most loving people you have ever met, but not many people come to the town of Eden anymore. The town is lost in their thoughts and in their hearts with every setting of the sun.

There were two special little children who had been born in the town of Eden, they were called Arty Grape and Mr Fox and they knew nothing else apart from the town that surrounded them. They were completely under the control of their parents who would cast a different spell every day. Their mama or papa could have told them that nothing else existed beyond the trees, and that a cat was really a dog or the sun revolved around the earth. Imagine believing something as silly as that? We all know the sun is a figment of our collective imagination.

Arty Grape and Mr Fox were two of the lucky unlucky ones. In the town of Eden possibilities were endless, you could see who you were and who you wanted to eventually be – but not only that, you could choose the world you wanted to live in by simply imagining it. Time in the town of Eden is the main commodity exchanged, because we still haven't discovered how to sell time yet, just pieces of it. Mark my words, one day somebody somewhere will discover how to sell *actual* time and then we'll be in trouble. Let's just say time is important and shall remain important throughout this story, we will waste it and we shall discover more about it whilst it plays its dirty tricks on us.

Everything in the town of Eden was, or at least seemed to be perfect, and when everything is too perfect it tends to raise suspicions in the eyes of the suspicousnessenessone. Arty Grape was too young to be of a suspicious disposition, but she was at least a very curious person and a clever little thing.

She had become curious about everything in the world around her. She would wonder why the sky was blue and marvelled at the moon in the dark night. She would question everything, anything and everyone. She had even wondered where her dreams had come from and if you could record them just like recording her favourite visual show. Curiosity never killed any cats, curiosity made the cat wonder why it *was* a cat. Arty Grape had many curiosities, her biggest curiosity, and forgive me for not mentioning it earlier, was a monolithic building that stood towering over the hill in the not so distant distance.

Arty Grape often wondered about this building, she could see it from her bedroom window at night, but at the end of this story she never saw it again.

It sat there motionless, like buildings usually do. It had zero windows that stretched from its top to its bottom, there were no doors and there was no way of gaining access to its insides. Despite its size on the beautiful landscape, it was as if it didn't exist. Why didn't it exist you may be asking? Well, it was because nobody spoke of it and nobody ever acknowledged its presence. Even when Arty Grape would ask about it she would never get the answer she needed. It was gone and forgotten; but it did exist and Arty Grape could not remove it from her mind. It had become burned into her memory. She wanted to know what it was and why it was there, but most of all she wondered how she could get there. At first she thought she could catch a train from the station in Eden, but she had never seen a train arrive or depart on yesterday, today or tomorrow. The town didn't welcome any trains anymore, and the tracks had become dusty and old.

I'm not sure about you but I'm a little curious, not only about the town or the tower, but about Arty Grape and Mr Fox. I mentioned they were two special little children and I forgot to tell you why...Arty Grape and Mr Fox were the only children left in the town of Eden after all the others had disappeared. I'll be following Arty Grape and Mr Fox to the tower on the hill, and I hope that you will follow me through these pages too.

We shall leave on the call of the eagle.

Let Me Introduce Me

No matter what you may think or whatever ramblings occur, this story is all about Arty Grape & Mr Fox, so I think it's only polite to introduce them both now. I am using Arty Grape and Mr Fox as a deflection from myself and I try to hide myself from as many people as I can, but I too am buried in these pages for you (never) to find. You will never really know who I am – but who you think I am will be with you for some time. They say that time moves along a singular path but in this story it takes on a different form, you'll understand what I mean around page forty-seven-and-one-half. The time I spend with you will be longer than the time you spend with me, if that makes any sense to you. But trust me when I say I do make sense, it's just my sense is like a jigsaw puzzle, you never get the pieces in the order you expect.

I am the one telling this story, it is my voice that you hear in your head and these are my words that I have placed among these pages, some to confuse you, others to lead you down my garden path. I have ears like the eyes of a hawk; I am always listening even when you think I'm not. I am buried deep within this story and you will never figure out the parts of me that I'm wanting to give away. Did some of the things we will talk about happen to me, or in my mind?

Did they happen to Arty Grape or Mr Fox? Are these real people or are they figments of my twisted imagination? Does it really matter? They merely grace these pages of deception and then they will disappear when the last page is turned and you have rolled over to sleep, perchance to dream.

Arty Grape was a beautiful young girl. I can't tell you her age because I don't know what it is, my imagination keeps changing it. Arty Grape had more than beauty; she was clever, funny, contemplative and kind. Most of all, Arty Grape was filled with unanswered questions of curiosity, she was always thinking and she was always talking. Arty Grape's hair was the colour of the nicest piece of brown toast you could ever eat; it burst into the atmosphere every day upon awakening. If you were to unwrap it from its prison and pull it ever so slightly, it would stretch down to her knees and then bounce back up again. She was tall and slim. She had a ballerina's build and she liked to dance like a ballerina too. Her favourite foods were fruit and salad, and on occasions she couldn't stuff enough mango chutney into her mouth. Arty Grape was a caring person with a natural motherly way, or fatherly for that matter (let's get that straight right now). Each new day her eyes revealed a different colour to the world, they changed from blue to green depending on her mood and depending on the light that surrounded her. (There is a scientific fact behind eyes changing colour like hers you know, there's an actual reason to that fact; unfortunately it's over there behind that chair).

Arty Grape didn't know what colour her eyes were because there were no mirrors in her comfortable abode or at least no mirrors that she could reach to gaze into. Arty Grape would occasionally ask her mama and papa what colour her eyes were, but they would lie to her and tell her something different each time. She would often wonder what she looked like, at times she would catch her reflection in some surface and she would stand and stare, she would try to figure out who she was and she would wonder if she was a good person or a bad person.

Arty Grape's very best friend was her brother--Mr Fox. They would do everything together, as brothers and sisters should when they are young. Arty Grape was older than her brother and she took great care of him, like a bird that first looks after its young and then throws it out of the nest to plummet to its possible death, just like that. Arty Grape and Mr Fox would play games in their bedroom at night, making the expected amount of noise that children tend to make. It didn't matter about the noise, it mattered that they were spending quality time together. Little did they know what that time would eventually mean.

Nobody knew what was going through the mind of Arty Grape, it was like trying to read the mind of any other person, which we all know is only possible sometimes. All I can tell you is this -- the cogs were turning and the wheels were moving all the time, those cogs never stopped. One thought would lead to the next thought and that thought to another, it was a beautiful curse that only some are afflicted with. There was something special about Arty Grape, let me give you an example: She could think about a movie in her mind that she hadn't seen for a very long time, and remember her mind is the most secret of all the places. After she thought about a movie it would appear on the visual screen within the next few days, she would then sit and watch it with a big smile on her face, a really creepy smile that disturbed everyone that looked upon it. Sometimes she would be thinking about something very random and hours later overhear other people talking about the same thing. A coincidence you might say or was there another hidden explanation?

Before I forget, I want to leave you with a very different kind of thought. At this very moment in time the earth is spinning at one thousand miles per hour and travelling around the sun at sixty-seven thousand miles per hour. Every planet and every moon is kept in the right place because at some point in time the universe just formed. The weirdest thing about this fact is that we accept it for the way it is. Does this seem logical to you? Don't get me started on the sun, that massive ball of fire that is the precise amount of distance away for life to survive on Earth. If these kinds of things don't bother you then you must know something that I don't, and you're probably not going to like this story.

Look at me, I've already started rambling, I didn't think I rambled until later on but I'm doing it all the time, if I were you I would try to get used to it now.

Let us not forget about Mr Fox. He is yet another beautiful creature in this story of things. I've never really had to think about Mr Fox before now. When I started this story he didn't even exist, he wasn't even a figment of my imagination, but here he is, alive and well, making his mark in other people's lives. When you looked upon Mr Fox you knew who he was going to be, it had already been written in the scrolls of his life, which resided on a dusty bookshelf in the time library. Mr Fox didn't know who he was going to become yet, he still walked around with a blissful innocence inside of him. He resonated an inner peace that others could see and feel. He was calm, cool and collected: nothing fazed him and he would accept most things that came his way. Mr Fox didn't like to talk as much as Arty Grape but he thought as much as she did, in his quiet little way. He was as clever, if not cleverer than her. He would learn everything and more from his sister, as she would slowly teach him many of her wonderful ways. His skin was the colour of milky chocolate. His hair was as wild as he wanted it to be. He was the type of person who would do well in life without trying to conquer it. Aren't we all trying to conquer it? If not life then something else. Mr Fox... Mr Fox... What a lovely boy he was. Was he more like his mama or more like his papa? He was of course a combination of them both, but what that combination was couldn't be calculated. He was handsome, he was kind, he was a cool dude. Mr Fox... Mr Fox. He was a quiet kind of enigma waiting to be solved. Was he a puzzle or was he just Mr Fox?

Arty Grape and Mr Fox were two people but really they were one. They were similar to each other and at the same time as different as could be. They both had their own way of looking at the bright and beautiful world and together they made it seem less scary than it actually was, they gave you everlasting hope.

If you would be kind enough to indulge me, we shall follow these two beautiful creatures from the very start to the very end. They will never leave us, I promise you they will always be there, whether in my memory or yours, whether they stand next to each other or if they get lost momentarily. I, too, am also hoping to find out a little bit more about them, all the wonders that they have in store for me. Even though I am writing this story, they are writing me.

One day I met a large man and he had a large dog by his side. As the evening progressed I asked him a simple question: 'I'm not sure who is following who?' said I. 'Am I following you or are you following me?'

'We're both following the dog, and even he doesn't know where he's going,' replied the large man.

The NoWhereMan

Oooooooh dear me. These rambling thoughts are making me forget the order of things. I've realised I have forgotten to introduce you to the NoWhereMan. I'll probably do that quite a lot, forget things that is, and get everything muddled up. I have so many things to remember and write down that even the NoWhereMan has become lost in me too. Where had the NoWhereMan gone? Let's start with who he is.

The NoWhereMan always portrays himself as something other than who he is. He never wants people to know who he truly is or where he originally came from. He gives a different name to people each time they ask; he dons different outfits at different periods of time. He was once a man with no name but temporarily he is a man of no place that you or me could ever imagine. He is very important to this story even though he doesn't appear in it as much as you think he should. He likes to blend into the background of the tapestry of life, like a *Ghost Dog*. He behaves in a peculiar way or a way you may find peculiar. He is strange but never creepy. To many he was as normal and as sane as the next person, this was his great trickery that he carried in his little box. The NoWhereMan, like Arty Grape, would wonder and wander the streets of Eden. If you don't wander and wonder then what else is there to do? He would walk around the town of Eden until a clock spoke two twenty-two, and then he was gone until the next day or until the next time he was seen. Nobody knew where he had vanished to, nobody had taken the time to ask him; nobody had thought to ask his name and nobody really knew he was wearing a disguise, a disguise to trick them into thinking something else. It's very easily done, you know: I'm wearing one right now and I pray that you never find out what's behind it.

The NoWhereMan always wore a large and heavy looking coat, it cleverly hid his face from the world around him, he wore thick blue gloves even on the hottest of the summer days. (This is what led me to believe that he must have been insane because what sane person does that? What person walks around talking to themselves in the daylight for everyone else to see?)

The NoWhereMan walked the town each day, he would look around and observe but nobody knew he was an observer. You would always hear him before you saw him, he pushed an old ladies shopping trolley around with him and you could hear the wheels trundle with every one of his dirty steps. Who knows what was in his trolley, not a single person ever asked or wanted to ask. Arty Grape thought it was something different every time she laid her eyes upon it, she would let her imagination run wild. One day she thought it was full of cute little kittens, sweets, chocolates, chocolate biscuits and sometimes the ears of dead strangers that he had met on Monday, Tuesday and Gaaajuberday. Arty Grape being the curious girl that she was wanted to find out more about him and the only way to do that was to ask him some questions.

Before we continue where we left off, which I think was when Mr Fox was drowning in the river... Hold on, wait a minute, we were somewhere different weren't we, were we? It doesn't matter. Let's be honest with ourselves. You've read this far and you haven't put the book down yet, I'm not certain, where is that book now? Where did you leave it? Is it by the side of your bed? Is it on your floor? Pick it up and read it god damn you, I've not finished with you yet!

I'm trying not to ramble, I really am. I'm still trying to finish off telling you who the NoWhereMan is or at least what he told me. I know he wasted a lot of time, he had wasted time doing this, he had wasted time doing that, and he had wasted time doing everything else. He had met so many people along his way and he had a lot more people to meet. There were long periods of time when the NowWhereMan had liked meeting people, talking to them, discovering things about them so he could understand his own place in the world, looking for any kind of reflection in another to validate himself and his own existence. Does this sound similar to you? This reflection that he sought was to be found in other people – whether in person, in books, in music or in different dimensions. He eventually realised that he wasn't alone and that everything he thought was pointless energy: ones and zeros, atoms and particles floating through the air. Was it energy he was sub-consciously seeing in other people or was it energy that drew him towards certain people more than others? He didn't know but he enjoyed finding it out, he had nothing else to do other than observe what was happening around him. People are strange yet beautiful. 'Hi my name is James Joshua Jones, nice to meet you, how do you do?' Nothing mattered to him, especially names, he just existed and he just flowed into people's lives before flowing out of them again. Would his thoughts be transmogrified, diluted then watered down? The NoWhereMan had listened to people talk and talk, they revealed things to his trusting nature. He would be pulled like a magnet to all the genuine people of his time and of his place; he would feed from their stories, adding them to his own but one day he decided to stop talking to people and he decided to stop listening to their stories because they had stopped listening to him. Their selfish needs overcame them and there were very few that could engage in conversation anymore. This was when the NoWhereMan began to observe from a greater distance, to see what other things they would reveal with their silent language. His new method of exploration brought unexpected delights; he would leave his old ways behind him.

The NoWhereMan will appear from time to time and in very different places, but he has no real purpose in this story, unless you give him one. Was he an unexpected guide, a shining star that people would follow to the ends of the earth? If you looked at the NoWhereMan you would never think to follow him and he never thought people should either. Why would you follow anyone if they could lead you down a path that wasn't of your own making? Just like the place I hope to take you, that place is my mind on paper. Have you ever tried to explain your mind? I recommend you avoid doing so.

No Mans Land

Arty Grape knew she had to talk to the NoWhereMan, he was
the only person in the town of Eden that didn't belong. He
must have come from outside the town, and he must have
something to say and strange stories to tell. Arty Grape didn't
know when she was going to meet him, but one day she
knew she would. Maybe he had come from the tower on the
hill she thought. If you stick with me I promise I won't tell
you later.

One day Arty Grape was wandering around the time of
Eden. Nobody knew where she was going; she didn't even
know where she was going. She stopped to look at all the
sights that there were to see and she listened to the sounds
moving through the air. It was on this day that she found
herself standing next to the NoWhereMan, unexpectedly and
right on time.

Arty Grape had become bored playing in her garden so she
had decide to leave it, and the only way to do so was to climb
down the muddy bank at the end of the garden to the path
below. It was such a treacherous way to go, over the edge of
the path revealed a long drop down to the river, one mis-step
and she would find herself falling forever. (At the edge of
everyone's world lies the wishes you don't want to come

true).

The rain began to fall as she walked into the town, but that didn't matter – her destiny was in front of her. She didn't know what was going to happen. Every time that Arty Grape stepped outside of her front door recently strange things would occur, things that you couldn't explain, things that you didn't understand or want to. Today Arty Grape was seeking the NoWhereMan but she didn't know it, in Arty Grape's mind she was just going for a little walk to curb her boredom, but her sub-conscience was guiding her now and forever, it was talking to her, telling her where to go, the thing nobody really believes exists because it can't be seen. She rambled around the town and without even realising it she found herself standing next to the NoWhereMan. She had stopped for a moment to give her aching legs a moment to rest and there he was or there he had appeared to her. He didn't look at her and he didn't speak but the NoWhereMan knew she was there. He was watching all the people as they passed, as they moved around and busied themselves, as they pretended not to see him. He stood in the rain looking strange to all those around him. Arty Grape stood there with him, getting wetter and wetter with every drop of rain that fell. She did what the NoWhereMan did, she embraced every drop of rain; she bathed in it until she felt cleansed. Several minutes passed before the NoWhereMan stepped backwards and took shelter under the awnings of the shops. Arty Grape stepped back and joined him too.

'Hello,' said Arty Grape. Trying to sound confident with her voice.

'Hello,' replied the NoWhereMan. His voice was deep, crackly and quite disturbing. He growled, groaned, grouched and grumbled his words – another one of his many disguises.

'What's your name?' Arty Grape asked.

'I'll tell you my name but first you have to tell me yours.'

'I'm Arty Grape.'

'Are you now, Arty Grape? I think you think you're Arty Grape because that's what you've been told.'

Arty Grape didn't know how to respond to that, so she said the only thing she could: 'What does that mean?'

'Aaaaah Haaaaaa haaaaaaaaah haaaaaaaaaaaaaaaaaaa,' laughed the NoWhereMan. He laughed so hard his body shook. He was clearly insane. 'It doesn't matter. So what can I do for you Arty Grape?

'Do you know what that tower on the hill is over there?' she asked.

'I don't see a tower, all I see are the hills,' he growled at her.

'I thought you'd say that,' she said.

'Well. If you see a tower, then why don't you find out for yourself what it is? I don't see this tower you talk of but I'll follow you when you decide to take me there. By the way, it's not the tower on the hill. It's the tower of the hill.'

Had the NoWhereMan slipped in his own deceit? thought Arty Grape. *He said he couldn't see it, yet he knows it by another name.* 'So you can see it?' she thought out loud.

'As I said Miss Grape, I see no tower on the hill.'

'Okay. Do you see the tower of the hill?'

'Of course I do, I'm not blind,' he sarcastically replied. It was several moments before Arty Grape realised the NoWhereMan had stopped disguising his voice; he now sounded like a gentle man, despite his scary and unusual appearance.

'Do you know how to get there?' Arty Grape asked.

The NoWhereMan paused for a moment and tapped his temple several times. 'Just follow the voices in your head, they will eventually take you to where you want to go.'

Once again Arty Grape didn't know how to respond to his answer so she said nothing, and she watched the rain continue to fall and the water slip away into the secret sewers under the street.

The clock in the town struck two twenty-two and the rain suddenly stopped. It was time for the NoWhereMan to leave. 'It is time for me to go now Arty Grape, but I am sure we will meet again in this story of yours. Our paths will cross on the way to the tower of the hill.'

And just like that, he was gone.

Arty Grape had made up her mind, she had to climb the mountain. It was a mountain of and in her own mind. She had procrastinated about it for far too long, she had to find out why it was there, she had to find out why all the children in the town of Eden had disappeared once upon a time (don't think she hadn't noticed they had gone). A seed had been planted and she wondered if it would grow, would it flourish into a tall plant that bares wondrous fruit? If it does then don't let the neighbours look after it.

Once again I need to apologise, I've got myself muddled up as I've written this. There was something I needed to tell you. It happened in the morning twenty-three days ago – in fact it was the twentieth day of the thirtyoneth month. Mr Fox and Arty Grape were being subdued by one of the many visual screens once again. Papa decided it was time to turn them off; it was time for them to think for themselves, to turn their brains back on.

'SHUT IT DOWWWWN!' Papa commanded in a deep voice.

'But it's nearly...'

'SHUT IT DOWN NOW!' he bellowed once again, staring scarily at Arty Grape like she was his enemy, before flashing a smile at her, letting her know he wasn't serious, but was. It was then that Arty Grape decided to ask the question that she hadn't asked for a very long time. Papa prepared them breakfast and they sat at the kitchen table to eat. Mr Fox sat next to her munching and day dreaming about the universe; he thought about the pictures he had seen of neurones in his brain had looked similar to the pictures of the galaxy. He pondered for a moment, thinking about how he must have his very own universe inside his head.

'Papa. What's that tower on the hill?' Arty Grape bravely asked.

'What tower?' wondered Papa.

'That tower there,' she said pointing through the window at the tower on the hill. It sat there directly in front of her finger and directly in from of her papa too.

'What tower? Arty I'm not in the mood for games today. You keep asking the same question and playing the same game with me, but I'm not playing it anymore.'

'Paaaapaaaaaaaaaaaaa? That tower there, you can see it, can't you?'

'There's nothing there Arty, all I can see are the beautiful hills and the green trees.'

'Paaaapaaaaaaaaaa? she questioned once again.

'Okay! Thats enough now Arty. I don't want to play this game anymore!' The question that Arty Grape had always asked had been answered in a way she had come to expect, which is why she hadn't asked it for a very long time. It was a futile question with a futile response. Nobody could answer her questions, she had to figure it all out for herself. She had been asking people about the tower on the hill at every opportunity she had, but at every opportunity they had all denied its existence. The only person who believed it was there was her brother, but she had begun to wonder if they had been sharing the same hallucination. Was it just a part of her imagination, was her mind playing some kind of trick? Had the tower on the hill become the same as the voices in her head, the voices that she could hear from time to time, the voices that spoke to her? How did the NoWhereMan know that she heard those voices she wondered?

Are you still with me?

That question isn't directed at you; I'm asking myself the question the voices are asking me. I'm checking that I'm still with myself and I haven't wandered off somewhere that I shouldn't be.

Meet The Family Part Seven Eight Six

It was morning in the household and everything was silent, even the mouse. Arty Grape's papa and mama were in bed, as they usually were at 7:00am on a Saturday morning. Who wants to get out of bed at that time, I ask you? I'll tell you who, shall I? It's those people who don't love a bit of bed. Arty Grape often wondered if her mama and papa pretended to be asleep when she entered the room. Sometimes she would see them throw their bodies back down against the mattress and make what sounded like pretend snoring noises.

Mama and Papa loved to sleep – when you have children sleep becomes as precious as gold, but if somebody were to ask you if you wanted sleep or gold, you would of course choose gold. Or would you? Imagine if you had all the gold in the world, but you didn't have sleep. That doesn't sound pleasant now does it?

Arty Grape and Mr Fox walked into the bedroom as they usually did, it would always be a funny sight to witness. They would wake up and instantly rise from their beds, like time vampires, and walk in to Mama and Papa's bedroom. They could barely see as they walked because of the mushy sleep still trapped in their eyes. They would automatically navigate their way across their room, stepping over all the things that lay there from the night before: the mess they had created yet couldn't see.

Today was a day when Mama and Papa weren't pretending to sleep, they had been awake for some time and they were talking to each other about this and that. When Arty Grape and Mr Fox entered they immediately sat up and greeted them.

'Good morning Butt Face, good morning Puke Head, how are we on this fine morning?' Papa playfully said.

'Good.' Arty Grape murmured.

'Good.' Mr Fox said, as he yawned himself awake.

Arty Grape and Mr Fox were getting used to being born again. It was a new day, they didn't really know where they were or what was happening for the first few moments of their arrival.

'Please place your arm under the blue light and your new identification will be given to you momentarily.' Papa said.

Arty Grape hadn't left her dream world yet, and she was processing what was real and what was a figment of her brilliant imagination. Mr Fox jumped on the bed and worked his way under the covers, wriggling his way slowly but surely to comfort between Mama and Papa, Mr Fox had inherited his parents love of bed. Toby and Tiger were tucked tightly under his arms. Arty Grape assumed her position and sat on the red chair by the desk, it had become her throne. They pondered what to watch today on the visual screen, in the room, and they both thought about breakfast: it was the two toughest decisions they would probably face on this great day. Like clockwork they both sat and argued over what to watch.

'Fox, do you want to watch this?' Arty Grape asked rubbing her eyes.

'No.'

'What about this?'

'No.'

'This?'

'No.'

'Ooooh Fox, what do you want to watch? Papaaaaaaaa, everything I've suggested to Fox he doesn't want to watch,' she grumbled.

'Okay you two. If you can't decide what you want to watch, I'm going to choose for you or turn it off,' said Papa. The day had now started and the day wouldn't be his own until they were back in bed again.

'What about this one Fox?' asked Arty Grape.

'Okay,' he said.

They sat silently and they relaxed watching something that they both enjoyed, it was only when hunger set in did they think to speak.

'Papa, I'm hungry,' Arty Grape complained.

'It's your turn babe, I did breakfast yesterday,' he responded, turning to Mama with a smile on his face.

'Okay, what would you two like?' she sighed. Papa would have sighed too if it was his turn, there was nothing more painful to him than getting out of bed.

'Can I have some grapes, apple, yoghurt and a bowl of Cheerios without milk please?' asked Arty Grape.

'Can I have a bowl of Cheerios with milk please?' said Mr Fox.

'Okay, give me five minutes and I'll go and do it,' Mama responded.

Five minutes came and went and no breakfast had appeared for the children, Mama and Papa were still putting the world in its place, conversing with each other and enjoying each other's time together.

'Mama, can you do our breakfast now please?' Arty Grape begged.

'Okay. I'm going,' she said, sighing once more. She peeled herself from the bed, wrapped herself in her grey leopard patterned dressing gown and disappeared upstairs.

Whilst she was gone, Papa decided that this was the right time to talk and annoy Mr Fox, he turned to give him a cuddle. 'You okay Mr Fox?' Papa said, 'Did you sleep okay?'

'Yeah.'

'Did you dream?'

'Yeah?'

'What did you dream about?'

'I can't remember?'

'You can't remember?'

'No.' Mr Fox had already lost his focus and he kept turning his head to the visuals that had become the drug of his time.

'Okay Mr Fox, if you can't tell me what you dreamt about, maybe you shouldn't have any more visual time today,' Papa joked.

'Nooooooooo. You're joking?' protested Mr Fox.

'Nope. Unless you can tell me what you dreamt about then there is no visual time for you today,' Papa said, with a smile on his face again.

'Uuuuuhhhm. I dreamt I could fly.'

'What, like Superman?'

'Yeah, I was flying over all the tall buildings, looking down.'

'Looking down? Did you think to yourself just how small everything is and we are?'

'Yeah.'

'What happened next?'

Mr Fox was gone, he was lost in the visuals again and Papa realised trying to talk with him was getting him NoWhere, so he rolled back over and released Mr Fox from the conversational hold he had had on him.

Not long after he had rolled over did Mama return with

the breakfast feast for the children. Everything that they had asked for was there and it came with a side of freshly juiced juice and a variety of chopped fruit. They tucked in to the food with their eyes glued to the visuals, laughing out loud at all the things they found funny. They had a joyful innocence that we all once had. Their laughter didn't stop until Papa told them to go upstairs and do something creative with their minds. Even though he loved his bed he would soon join them. 'Okay you two, let's go shall we? Upstairs, come on, lets go, lets go, lets go. Move it, move it, move it.'

'Okay, okay.' Mr Fox said, whilst painfully removing himself from underneath the covers and the warmth. They reluctantly headed upstairs, Arty Grape and Mr Fox went first whilst Mama and Papa enjoyed a bit of cuddle time.

Sometimes visuals were the only way to get Arty Grape to stop thinking, but she wasn't allowed to be glued to them all day. What would she do today, what would she say? It didn't matter to Arty Grape because she would think of something and she would have many questions to ask. She would always say whatever thought was new to her, and it was a delight to watch those thoughts happening for the first time.

Mr Fox and Arty Grape occupied themselves whilst they waited for Mama and Papa to come and join them. They drew, they read, and they constructed great shapes. It was a lazy day after all. Mama and Papa climbed the stairs slowly, Papa walked in to the living room and they had stopped playing, they had snuck back on to the visuals He knew he was in for a small fight getting them to put the screens down. What the children failed to realise was that they would never win, no matter how much they thought they would. Not just yet anyway, and not against their papa.

'Right, that's it.' Papa said, with a no-nonsense voice. 'Time to finish soon.'

They didn't listen, just like they usually didn't when they

were immersed inside technology.

Papa stood there and watched them not listening. They were fixated and transfixed; mesmerised by the magic. 'Five more minutes!' he shouted.

'Paaaaaapaaaaaaaa. Can you pause the timer in your mind please?' pleaded Mr Fox. His papa just laughed back at him, he thought it was a very clever thing to say.

'I like that saying Mr Fox. If I ever write a book I'm going to use that sentence. Anyway, how do you suppose I pause the timer in my mind? Five more minutes! Are you listening to me you two?' They both responded with a moan that was stereoised. He had given them his final warning but he would inevitably let them play for longer than five minutes, because he wanted some peace and quiet, because he wanted to converse with his love. The children stared at the visual screen and Mama and Papa continued the conversation they had left downstairs until he felt it was time for the children to switch of the mind numbing gadgets.

'WooooHooooWooooHooooWoooooHooooo'   Papa sirened. He turned the visuals off without even asking.

'Paaaapa. I was watching that,' Mr Fox grumbled.

'I know you were. But it's time to turn it off now.'

'Buuuuut, can we just finish that last one?' whined Arty Grape.

'No!'

It was time to put the machines down and learn how to be bored. Once they were allowed to be bored they began creating and then wondering. It was also time for Arty Grape to begin talking, and then not stop for the rest of the day. Papa knew that the next words out of Arty Grape's mouth would be: *Ooooh Papa. What should we do?* Mr Fox would always ask for something he wanted to play with from the rickety cupboard of imagination. He was a creative genius with all his different design tools. The things he created were mind-boggling. Arty Grape was the opposite of Mr Fox, she liked to question and to wonder about everything that surrounded her, Mr Fox would wonder to but he would wonder to himself and only when he was finally ready would he question with his words.

Arty Grape began to think and think, but the one thing she had forgotten to think about was herself, who she was, where she had come from, why she was exactly where she was, and what was her own reality in reference to all the other things that surrounded her? Arty Grape hadn't even begun to question her own existence yet or what reality really was, maybe I'm wrong, maybe she questioned *everything* in her own little way. Maybe I've just forgotten the way that children think. Those clever little creatures that are a mystery to ourselves even though we were once one just like them, a very long time ago. There are many things I've forgotten about – one day I forgot who I was and where I was for a split second in time. When I say one day, it's actually happened to me on more than one occasion.

Arty Grape and Mr Fox had a wonderful family, shouldn't all families be wonderful? Every single person in the family had their own problems, of course they had their problems, every family does. Whether big problems or small problems, they are still problems all the same. Their papa, well, lets just say he did his best to be as good to everyone as he possibly could – he was after all a flawed human being that failed many times along the way. Don't we all fail, no matter how hard we try? If we can get simple sums wrong then what makes us think we can get life right? Papa was a firm but fair man, or at least he liked to think that about himself. He was playful then serious, and on different occasions he liked to socially experiment with everyone around him, including his children. In his lifetime he had been called many things by many people: an enigma, outrageous, shy and a weirdo, and all those things were all true at the time they were spoken. I'd like to think that Arty Grape and Mr Fox really liked their papa, but would they ever know who he truly ever is or was, unless he told them? Just like he would only know them until a certain age and then never truly know them after that. *Such is life*, he thought. *Such is life*. He had decided to tell them everything before they even knew it. He would be open and he would be honest with them and he would see which garden path that led them and him down. He shared information with them but only when he thought they were ready to hear it. He would joke with them, dance with them, lie to them, trick them. And damage them emotionally, slowly and unintentionally over time.

Mama was a beautiful lady, and her face would light up a room when she smiled. She had a laugh that could be heard and identified from a distance over a crowded room. She was kind, caring, compassionate and most of all forgiving, but unfortunately she was a dark person inside because her thoughts had consumed her, they had taken over. Of course I'm only joking: she was the most wonderful of persons, too good really, and anyone in her life would be very lucky to have her there. Mama was beautiful in every possible way.

I won't lie to you in this story, I'll tell you as much of the truth as I can. In this story everyone is happy and Arty Grape and Mr Fox's family are a happy family too. Everyone in the household had learnt to treat each other with respect, they couldn't complain and they tried to appreciate what they had and not what they didn't. They willed happiness into their lives because they had been taught to. They all loved each other and it showed. Arty Grape was wonderful and so was Mr Fox, they loved each other and they hated being apart, so I've kept them together in this story for as long as I can.

Where are Arty Grape and Mr Fox going to take you? If

you follow the white rabbit it will lead you down the yellow brick road where the wizard who lies to you resides. If you fall towards *Wonderland* you will surely meet Dorothy, and if you accept the blue pill it will take you back to the end of the Matrix. I don't want to take you to any of these places that you've been to before; I'm just asking you kindly to follow Arty Grape, she is the only one who knows the way out of this story. It's like a maze made of white pages. Do you want to follow her, will you let her take you there? Once you arrive you will find she wants to take you somewhere else, on another journey that never ends. Let's go shall we? Let's journey into this magical land of my nonsense. Remember it's only magical if you allow it to be, otherwise it's not a very pleasant place to be – it will be confusing, disorientating and disappointing quite frankly.

Come with me and you'll see into a world of pure imagination, we'll begin with a spin into your imagination.

YtisouC

'What should we talk about, Papa?' Arty Grape asked out loud to herself. She wasn't really talking to her papa, she was just talking.

'You tell me. You're the one that wants to talk, so why don't you think of something to talk about?' he said, staring creepily at her. 'I know, let's talk about the fact that when you look deep into space, you are really looking back in time or at least that's what they say. I've never looked back in time before, have you Arty? I wonder what that feels like?'

It looked like Arty Grape wasn't listening but she was, she was just storing that thought for later. She was going to allow it to sit and settle first and then talk about it when her papa least expected it. 'Well, don't get annoyed, Papa. I assure you it's just a question,' she said and paused for a moment, she wondered if she should say what she was thinking. 'What's that tower that sits there on the hill?' she sheepishly asked.

'You'll find out soon enough Arty, just have patience; there's no point in trying to get there too quickly. If you rush there, then you'll discover that that place has already left you behind.' As usual her papa was lying to her, he didn't want to tell her The Truth. 'Some say it's full of monsters and dark spirits. Others say that it's the place you go to find no answers.' He stopped and stared directly into her eyes, staring right down to the bottoms of her feet. 'I'm just kidding with you. I have no idea what it is.' He stopped staring and gave her a loving smile. He just looked at her. He was trying to freak her out. He had played with her mind so many times that Arty Grape was slowly forgetting which way was up and which way was around and around. But he had revealed something to her for the very first time; he had told her some semblance of The Truth. For the first time he hadn't denied its existence.

Arty Grape always believed the tower existed even though every other person had denied it was there. Every person she had asked about the tower had told her what a lovely imagination she had; some people would pinch her cheeks or pat her on the head and many others would get annoyed and walk off without even giving her an answer. It didn't matter what reaction they had to the question, the outcome was always the same: they didn't see it or they didn't want to see it. Arty Grape became more determined to find out the purpose of the tower on the hill. She had sat for too long, staring at it through the windows in her bedroom. She often wondered if she was going insane, it had happened to many before her. It must have been there she thought, she could see it, she could feel it, and her brother could see it too but he didn't seem interested in talking about it, so that made her even more unsure. Arty Grape put the idea of her own insanity aside for one moment, and she decided the only way to find out if it existed was to go there. This is when her scheming began.

For the remainder of the day Arty Grape plotted without looking like she was plotting. To the un-trained eye it looked like she was dancing to the music that was playing through the house and singing to the words the music brought. She danced and danced, and she talked to herself (her favourite type of conversation) while round and round in her head fluttered the erasable blueprints of how to escape the house. The ideas in her mind floated past her in beautiful transparency. She thought of nothing else but the tower on the hill, until her thoughts turned against her, and they turned into fear. She thought about how scary the journey might be; she thought about getting lost in the mountains; she thought about her cold dead body being eaten by the wild animals that roamed the Forest of Doom. The big wide world suddenly became very scary to her, and we all know what a scary place it is out there. It's full of beasts of unimaginable cruelty that we have to push out of our minds, and only then do we see what a wondrous place it is to live one of our many lives not of our choosing.

Scheming, Scheming went her day; there was no distracting Arty Grape from her plans. *I must scheme, I must think, I must plan my escape!* she thought. What once was her home had now become a prison, a prison that wrapped its impenetrable walls around her. Arty Grape needed to escape from one impenetrable place to the other. She thought about her plans as cleverly as she could – she thought about all the things that could go wrong, not about all the things that could go right. Suddenly it came to her: she needed to do nothing. She needed to behave as normal as she possibly could.

It was *Le Dinner Day* and they would eat and watch a movie with popcorn and sweets. Even though it was one of Arty Grape's favourite days it seemed to drag on forever, there was no pleasure to be found in the hours that followed. They never left the house on *Le Dinner Day*, even if the sun was shining and it was hot outside. The sun would shine again another day her papa always thought, so it would never be missed. Everyone kept themselves busy in some way: Mama prepared a delicious feast in the kitchen, Mr Fox tried to beat his papa in his weekly game of chess and Arty

Grape continued to pretend that she had an interest in all the things around her, but she didn't, and she would never enjoy anything until the mystery she had created was solved. HERE

'What movie should we watch today Arty? It's your choice,' Papa asked.

Arty Grape didn't respond, she had tuned everything out and was sat on the floor staring at a wall. (There were four of them, so you and I don't know which one it was that she stared upon).

'Arty!' he said a little louder. 'What movie should we watch today?'

It took a moment for Arty Grape to realise she was still in the room and a question had been asked of her. 'I don't know. I don't mind. You choose something.'

'Really? Okay, I've got a good one that I think you'll both enjoy. I watched this movie when I was your age and I loved it. If you don't like it then I will sell you to some other people.'

'That's fine?' she said, ignoring his strangeness.

'That's fine! That's fine! I thought you'd be more enthusiastic than that.'

'Do we have sweets and popcorn?' Mr Fox asked.

'Of course we do,' Papa replied. 'How can we have *Le Dinner Day* without sweets and popcorn?'

'AaaaaaweSooooommme,' Mr Fox sang.

'Dinner you lot,' Mama shouted from the kitchen. 'Come and sit down.' Nobody listened to her so she had to shout three more times before everyone slowly made their way to the table., Papa was also guilty of not listening from time to time. He was after all; *not a perfect person.*

Mr Fox sat down and immediately jumped back up again to go to the toilet. He would always leave it until the food was served before relieving himself.

They all scoffed their food down but Arty Grape didn't feel

hungry, she usually finished before her brother but today she had hardly started by the time he had finished. Her brain didn't have time for sending digestive signals to her stomach, all her processes were taken over by her cunning plans.

'Come on Arty, hurry up, we want to watch the movie,' Papa said.

Arty Grape continued to eat slowly, pretending to enjoy every gruesome bite. Eventually she finished and they all made their way to the sofas and sat in front of the visual screen. Papa prepared the movie and then the movie began to play. She sat and she munched on her popcorn and sweets, the same delicious sweets she had on the previous movie day, but now they had become tasteless to her, there was no enjoyment left in the delicious treats. Arty Grape couldn't wait for the day to be over but she had to wait for her papa to utter those inevitable words that she used to hate: 'Okay. It's time for bed.' Arty Grape would never usually ask to go to bed; she always wanted to stay awake until sleep completely took over her body and she could fight it no more. Asking to go to bed would have been very suspicious indeed but all she wanted to do was to lie in her bed and plan her escape, without any distractions or appearing unusual.

Finally she could see it was beginning to get dark outside, the light filling the room had changed and everything had become dimly illuminated with a soft golden glow. It could only mean one thing, the sun was beginning to set in the west and it would be bedtime very soon. Arty Grape's papa had always used the light to tell the time and she knew the words she wanted to hear would follow soon.

'Okay. It's time for bed,' Papa said firmly. 'Let's clean your teeth.'

Arty Grape did what she usually did to keep up her pretence, she battled with him. She employed several different tactics of manipulation that could be used to delay bedtime. (She and Mr Fox would both add new methods each day to try and control and confuse, but it only worked for so long before they were sent down to their rooms.) Finally Arty Grape could stop pretending. Now she could continue to think without interruption, without looking like there was something on her mind. Hers was a face that could tell no lies.

She threw herself onto her bed and she thought and she thought, but she still couldn't come up with a plan. *How can I leave the house the house without Mama and Papa noticing* she thought. Arty Grape thought so much that her head began to hurt, she looked over to her brother and he had already fallen asleep. He loved his bed and he couldn't resist giving in to its splendour.

Don't you forget about Mr Fox. He is still here but he is lying dormant right now, he will be back, don't you worry.

Arty Grape's eyes became heavy and she could think no more. Slowly she began to drift towards her dreams and she journeyed to that special place between each world – a place where you are neither there or here, a calm place where you begin to float and leave your body behind. But before you leave your body you are thrust into another world that you have no control over, and it is so deep you are no longer who you thought you once were.

Life without pain has no meaning.

Deep Diving

Everything turned black and all sounds had become a forgotten memory. A faint face lingered in the distance, and at the same time it was very close and clear to see. The face morphed into many alternative faces, some known and some unknown. Friends, family and strangers appeared; everything slowly and gently transformed into something else, it happened ever so slowly that it tricked the eye. The faces weren't hiding their identities, it was the mind that couldn't keep up with the imagery placed in front of it. It was fascinating to watch until the very end of its transformation, where all is revealed in the final act. The face slowly morphed into a shape that you dread to acknowledge, and when it arrives it is the shape of your inner demon, the demon of all. It has an elongated head and its razor sharp teeth scowl at you whilst its eyes look hungry. It longs to tear the flesh from your body, it is the only thing it enjoys doing anymore, nothing can satisfy its deviant ways. Tearing flesh apart excites this beast that preys upon you. As it moves closer towards you its mouth opens wider until it swallows you whole and you fall deeper and deeper. Wispy and smoky images enter your thoughts and these images change who you are forever. These are the things that lay deep and dormant, the thoughts that can never be, the thoughts that want to be forgotten. In this new beginning all manner of things show themselves: colours bursting like nuclear explosions, dogs barking, flowers blooming, falling to your death, a never-ending death. It is the strangest of places because you don't know where you are, or if you are you. Only when you realise where you are can you find some peace in the knowing. The deeper you go the stranger things become and the more you remember. Flashes of things once passed haunt you, and from this moment onwards you constantly wonder what they mean. *Why did I see those things? Where did they come from?* Deeper and deeper you fall, and as you fall there is a sign that points to a place you can never get to, a place where everyone is happy. Further and further you fall, passing the place where Arty Grape would usually wake up, but Arty Grape doesn't wake up; she wouldn't wake up for a very long time. Arty Grape continued to dream, immersing herself in her own subconscious where people played the roles of an infinite number of random choices of random people. Life in your dreams becomes a stage of your own abyss. How deep you travel into this abyss is of your own choosing.

It was in her dreams that Arty Grape saw the tower on the hill for what it really was. She found herself at the base of its magnificence. It stood far and wide and it didn't even bother to look at her, she was insignificant to its will. The tower was surrounded by beautiful trees that gently swayed without the help of the wind; and the trees danced without music, because they wanted to dance. The sky around it was a soft shade of pink and the clouds looked as if they were going to cry. Even in her dreams Arty Grape was drawn to the tower on the hill. There was no escape and she didn't want to escape it, she wanted to become part of it. Darkness fell around her, and beneath her feet lay a white floor that stretched into the black horizon. Two voices communicated in whispers behind her. She could only listen to them, she couldn't turn around to see who they were because Arty Grape no longer possessed a body, she had become part of her mind. Only then did she realise she was dreaming, everything had been so real up until that moment. It didn't feel like a dream, it felt like she had been there before and she would find herself there again soon. These were her visions of the future.

The images and the whispers stayed with Arty Grape until she woke from her current dream. She opened her eyes and looked up at the ceiling. She lay on her bed contemplating how many other dreams she hadn't awoken from? The whispers in her dreams stayed with her and they became the voices in her head that lived with her forever. They would never hurt her but they created a lifetime of wondering. It was these voices that had spoken to her, and they had told her to go the tower on the hill. Maybe these voices lived at the tower, she thought, and if she went there she would finally meet them.

Mr Fox is awake now but we're not venturing into his dreams just yet, we're venturing into mine. But my dreams are the dreams of Arty Grape, and her dreams belong to somebody else.

Where is Arty Grape going to take us?

The Holistic Approach

Arty Grape opened her eyes, and she was relieved to find herself in her bed and in her room. There had been many times when Arty Grape had woken up in a different place to where she had rested her head. She never knew how she got there, and she had stopped thinking it was odd – but again that's a different story for a different dimension of time. She had hoped that her dreams would have revealed a plan, but they didn't. She still had no way of escape. Her thoughts were stuck on a train track, they sped down the rails and they wouldn't get off until a solution to her problem was found.

Arty Grape climbed out of her bed and staggered around the room. She looked for her slippers and dressing gown before she wandered upstairs. She daydreamed her way into the living room and found the cosy blanket from behind one of the sofas and sat down. She needed to gather her thoughts, they were still travelling back from her dream world and they had yet to reach her. She sat and she stared at the black visual screen, where a distorted and faded version of herself was reflected back to her. Was that really her? Did she look like a faded ghost to everyone else? *How can I get out of this prison?* she thought. Arty Grape puzzled her own question for a while before she gave up and turned on one of the many visual screens, but she hadn't given up on giving up. Arty

Grape had decided to let the answer percolate to the surface without trying to seize it from her depths.

Arty Grape could hear Mama and Papa walking up the creaky stairs, they had decided to grace her with their presence. Mr Fox had decided to rise from his comfortable slumber and join her too. He never liked first thing in the morning, and it would take him a while to fully awake.

Soon it was time for breakfast and they chose their desires, which would change all the time, and today their desires had indeed changed once again. Arty Grape had fallen in love with runny honey on toast and wanted to drizzle honey on everything. If you ask me, I think she would cover her own foot in it and then eat it in a few large bites.

'I luuurve honey,' she drooled.

'I luuurve this,' drooled Mr Fox.

'Imagine if your bed was made out of breakfast Fox, all different shapes and sizes of things, and your pillow was so soft because it was filled with thick runny honey.'

'I would love that Arty,' said Mr Fox, with his eyes widening with every thought. 'I would so eat my bed.'

'Me too!' shouted Arty Grape, with her high amount of enthusiasm.

'I would cover my whole face in honey and spend all day licking it off... mmmmmmmmmm. That would be so niiiiiiiiiiiiicccce.'

'Mmmmmmmmmmm. Yeeeeaaaaaah. Soooooo Niiiiiiice.'

This is how breakfast usually went. Arty Grape and Mr Fox conversed about anything and everything, the most silliest of things that we often forget. They weren't concerned about the affairs of the morning news, or the price of pumpkins; they would use their imaginations constantly and consistently. They would think strange yet wonderful things that no adult bothered to think about anymore. They created temporary worlds where they could joyfully live. Imagine one of those worlds if you can, because they do exist in a hidden place.

Arty Grape and Mr Fox carried on eating, talking and imagininating until the music started. Their little ears were blasted by the sounds from history – it was time for them to dance and shake their booties. Arty Grape and Mr Fox moved in their own delightful ways and Mama and Papa joined them in the dancing, they shook their booties in the most embarrassing ways.

'Shake that booty Fox,' shouted Papa over the music. 'Yeah baby!' Mr Fox shook his bootylicious booty. 'Great moves my man, shake it, shake it,' he shouted again. Arty Grape started singing to the song. 'Sing it sister!' Papa shouted at Arty Grape. 'Sing it!' Arty Grape belted out the words to the song, clenching her fist to use it as a microphone. They danced without a care in the world.

It was time for some classical music next. Papa started waving his hands like he was born a conductor – at least he thought he was a born conductor, he was really just a maniac throwing his arms around in the air, blindly and badly, for his own amusement. 'Da Da Da Daaaaaa. Da Da Da Daaaaaaaa,' Papa shouted.

'Banannnnna Naaaaaaa. Banannnnna Naaaaaaa,' Arty Grape shouted.

They danced and they danced until they were out of breath.

Mama and Papa collapsed in a heap on the sofa. 'Okay you two, you have to get dressed now.' Mama wheezed. It was time to tidy up and leave the house. It was time to head to the swimming pool but they had to navigate leaving the house first, which was never easy. Everyone would have to get organised and get ready. Mama would take hours, she had been given the title of the *slowest woman in the world*; Mr Fox and Arty Grape would get distracted by one thing or the other; and Papa would always be left waiting for everyone else.

Today was no different. The usual routine ensued and Papa was stood there waiting until they had finally finished their individual craziness. 'Come on babe, hurry up. We're all waiting,' he shouted down the stairs.

'Are we going yet?' asked Mr Fox.

'We're just waiting for Mama,' Papa said.

'Aaah, Mama is the slowest woman in the world,' Arty Grape said.

Papa laughed and shouted down the stairs again.

'I'm coming, I'm coming,' shouted Mama.

Finally they headed out of the house and they all walked hand in hand along the pavement, mama and papa carried their scooters heavily on their shoulders. Arty Grape was talking and Mr Fox was listening and processing everything that he saw and heard. They would play 'I Spy' as they walked and Mr Fox would always choose something that had long passed and couldn't be seen any more.

'I spy with my little eye, something beginning with phhhhhhhhhh,' spluttered Mr Fox.

'Face?' Arty Grape shouted confidently.

'No.'

'Feople?' Papa said.

'Feople? No,' he replied.

'Fence,' Mr Fox revealed.

'Where's the fence, I can't see a fence?' said Papa.

'Its back there, we just passed it.'

'Mr Fox, I have to be able to see it. You can't do that. Unless I can see it how am I supposed to guess what it is? ...Oh well, my turn now then. I spy with my little eye something beginning with *ell*.'

Everyone sat quiet for a little while, they all tried to think what it could be, the quietness didn't last long before they started shouting out random answers, even things they couldn't see. Arty Grape would always ask for clues and give up too easily. Mr Fox didn't care until it became his time to I Spy.

'Give me a clue, Papa!' Arty Grape begged.

'If I give you a clue you'll get it,' he always replied.

'Is it a plant?' she grumbled.

'Where can you see a plant? Tell me where you can see a plant? "Plant" doesn't begin with the letter *ell* either.'

'I give up,' she said, and then sulked.

'Me too,' said Mr Fox.

'It's lips,' said Papa.

'Aaaaaagh. My turn now,' Arty Grape burst out.

'Wooooaaaaaaah! You didn't get mine, if you want your turn you have to guess mine first.' This continued until they became bored and they didn't want to play any more.

'Do you want to go on your scooters for a bit?' asked Papa.

'Yes please,' replied Mr Fox.

'Yes please,' said Arty Grape. They both hopped on their scooters and scooted as fast as they could away.

They slowly worked towards the sea and to the swimming pool, talking as they travelled, the closer they were to the coast, the louder the squawks of the seagulls became. In the distance they could see the horizon of the sea and the sky. It was always a beautiful sight to see, even if the rain was falling hard and the sea was enraged, it would always look beautiful. Today the sea was calm, and when the sea was calm it had a serene turquoise colour, it wasn't a colour you would often see. They walked past the houses that were painted blue, pink, yellow or any colour you could imagine. If you were to look upon them they would put a smile on your face, one hundred percent of half the time.

Slowly and surely they made their way and when they arrived the fun began. They got changed as quickly as they could and they ran and jumped into the water. Papa chased them, and when he caught them he would pick them up and throw them into the deep end. They would always emerge from the water moments later screaming and spluttering. 'No, Papa, stop it!' Arty Grape would shout, but Papa would never listen. He grabbed her again and she screamed for him to let her go, but he didn't and he threw her in once more. They always used to hate it at first, but the more he did it, the more they enjoyed it and eventually they would emerge with smiles. They would swim around the pool, they would dive under water, they would throw themselves down slippery slides that looked gigantic next to them. Forwards, backwards and upside down they slid, it was pure freedom. Arty Grape and Mr Fox wanted to swim all the time, they wanted to live at the swimming pool. But we all know what happens when you live in the place you love don't we? I for one begin to dislike it. Let's see if evolution can continue to get rid of the many silly flaws that we have shall we?

Everything would always have to end, and leaving the swimming pool was always a disappointment for Arty Grape and Mr Fox. At least they had the showers to finish off their routine of fun. I think Mr Fox's favourite part had become the showers. He had his very own shower routine and dance, he would call it the *shower dance*. He loved the showers and he loved to dance. It was the dance of the *dream man*, and he found himself in his own world when he did it.

It was at the showers that Arty Grape was struck by a figurative bolt of lightning. *It's the weekend. Mama and Papa like to stay in bed as long as they possibly can on the weekend,* she thought to herself. She was right too, they would stay in bed as long as they could without actually starving their own children. Mama and Papa would stay in bed for as long as the joy outweighed the discomfort of needing the toilet. *If me and Mr Fox don't bother them, they won't come and bother us. If we're quiet they will be as quiet as they possible can be too. If we can be back before they even realise we've gone, everything will seem the same to them.*

Everything doesn't stay the same though does it? Everything changes all the time and all around us, whether we want it to or not, and everything would change for Arty Grape and Mr Fox. Tomorrow they would never return to their innocence again. It would be taken from them slowly in the most unpleasant of ways.

Right now it was time to go home and relax. Arty Grape was tired but buzzing with excitement. She wanted to play, create, talk and discuss, but her papa wasn't having any of it. Mama and Papa were tired so she had to play by herself and talk to herself once again.

Arty Grape and Mr Fox both played by themselves before they were allowed to turn to the visual screen, to see what answers it had with all its black magic. Mama and Papa sat and had a glass of their favourite juice and talked the evening away in the kitchen. When it was time, Papa prepared dinner and served it plate by plate before calling the children. They sat nicely and they talked about their day. They talked about many other days and many other memories. They giggled at all the silly things that had happened; like the time Arty Grape punched herself in the face which had left a bruise for days, and the time Mr Fox did fell and smashed his leg on the rope obstacle course.

Soon it would be time to sleep and time to wake up again. It would be time to get up and go. Arty Grape felt at peace because she was about to find out if the tower on the hill was real for the first time. She was going to touch it and she was going to find out what secrets it held.

Getting Up To Go

They say a journey begins with a single step but Arty Grape thought that was extremely silly. *Surely,* she thought, *it begins with breakfast.*If she was going to venture on any big trip she was going to need a large breakfast; one of her favourite breakfasts too. She craved for crunchy peanut butter on thick brown toasted bread. She loved the crunchy sound that it made with every bite.

That morning she woke up before the sun rose, it wasn't easy and she had to fight with herself just to roll over. Who wants to wake up before the sun rises? Gradually she opened her eyes – it took longer than she thought it would – and when her eyes were finally open she could hardly see, they had been glued together by that stuff, you know, the gunk that seems to come from nowhere. She fell out of bed and wandered around the room for a moment before she realised what she had to do... and what she was about to do. She needed to get dressed, but before getting dressed she needed to find her clothes. Arty Grape slowly wrestled her way around her room looking for all the items she needed. Arty Grape put on her woolly jumper and then her woolly jeans before finding her woolly hat and eating a woolly banana that she had found on the floor. Her face produced a smile as she put on her favourite pair of boots, her pink Doc Martin boots.

Not the bright girly pink that I know you're thinking about, but a 'special kind of pink' as her mama would call it: soft subtle and all grown up.

Her room was a mess. Various amounts of different-shaped things were littered across the floor, the chaos without the order. Drawings were scattered up the walls; there were books galore on multiple subjects; chess pieces laid strewn across the floor like they had been slaughtered on the black and white battlefield. It looked like the room of a mad woman. A page from a body language book had been torn from its home and it lay there looking up at her. The title on the page said 'Universal Gestures' and the words echoed out into the room. Her papa had given her the book just in case she wanted to read it.

Arty Grape continued to clamber around her room – standing up, crawling, and looking under the things that things were under – until finally she found everything she needed for her journey ahead. It was time and she was ready. And she was scared – scared because she knew herself very well. There was no way she would talk herself out of the task she had set herself. *To the death... No... To the pain!*

Arty Grape knew she was going somewhere, but she had never been to somewhere before and she wondered what it would be like. She paused for a moment and she drifted like she was about to dream again. She stood there, quite still, and she gazed into the space of her room and began to think about the tower on the hill. She closed her eyes and she felt a warmth grow inside of her. She saw herself floating over the green mountains. She saw all the people she had left behind, and she could see the tower in the distance. Arty Grape belonged at the tower and finally she was going home. It was time for her to go, so she crept out of her bedroom and up the stairs into the kitchen. When she arrived in the kitchen she found Mr Fox waiting, he was fully dressed and ready to go on the new adventure with her. He had already eaten his breakfast. He had scoffed down jam on a muffin, with a cheeky packet of crisps on the side for good measure.

'Morning Arty. You ready?' he said, smiling.

'What are you doing?' she barked back at him. 'Why are you awake?'

'I'm coming with you,' he said smiling once again.

'To school?' she said 'That's where I'm going.'

'To school on a Sunday?' Mr Fox answered back. 'Do you remember asking me to come? Do you remember what you told me?' he asked, with a curious look on his face.

'I didn't ask you to come, I didn't tell you anything.'

'Seriously! You told me everything just before you fell asleep. Don't you remember?'

'Okay, whatever, I haven't got time to argue with you. Come if you want but don't get in my way, annoy me or slow me down because I'm not waiting for you.' Arty Grape *had* told her brother everything and she *did* ask him to come with her but she couldn't remember, it was the start of the many things should would forget.

'I asked you what you were thinking about, I could see you staring at the wall and thinking,' said Mr Fox.

'You're telling me that you can see me thinking now? Okay whatever you say.' It was true, you could always see when Arty Grape was thinking, you would see a quiet look on her face, like waters that slowly calmed. Her eyes would stop moving at all the empty things she saw. She could sit like that for hours, until something brought her back from the other realms, snapping her out of her fugue. 'I don't remember that. I'll have some breakfast and we'll go,' she quickly said.

Mr Fox was ready, he had no idea how they were getting there and he had no idea what he would find. Mr Fox didn't let his imagination run wild like Arty Grape's, he just let whatever happened happen. He was more than happy to follow his sister.

Arty Grape quietly prepared her breakfast, and then she sat at the table and started eating. Everything was silent apart from the crunch of her biting into her toast. Each bite sounded one hundred times louder than usual. They both nearly burst into tears of laughter, so Mr Fox had to look away and out of the window, and as he stared into the dark of the night his ears registered the humming of the refrigerator. Its frequency meant it had melded into the background, insidiously entering his mind. Arty Grape crunched and crunched whilst listening to the silence. It felt like they were the only two people left in the world, like every other person had decided to leave this place and never come back. Why would they want to come back? It was a desolate place, void of any meaning.

'I'm ready,' Arty Grape whispered as she wiped the remnants of her breakfast from the side of her mouth. She had left just enough peanut butter on her lips for it to be a distraction to the people that had to look at her.

'Wipe your mouth,' said Mr Fox. 'You've got some peanut butter on it!'

Arty Grape wiped her mouth again, clearing the debris of food. 'Let's rock and roly poly!'

They slowly snuck out the front door (not the back door, that would be too obvious) and closed it as carefully as they could. They wanted to be like ninjas that crept through the night, unseen and unheard. They could have snuck out the back and followed the path at the end of the garden, but that path was a treacherous one. Arty Grape decided it would be wise to find the other hidden path in the town of Eden. They took the long cut instead of the short, and let me tell you now that they made the right choice. As they pulled the front door shut it felt like it made a loud noise, but really it only made a small click. Then they faced the main road for the first time on their own, looking both ways.

'Which way Arty?' Mr Fox asked.

Arty Grape looked left and right. To her right, the steep hill would lead her down to another hidden part of the world that she knew existed. To her left was a path that she had only been told about but never seen. One day as she had walked with her papa he had pointed, casually, and told her about a path at the start of the trees that led down to the river. 'Left,' Arty Grape said. She decided to find the path that she had never taken.

They walked along the side of the road hoping nobody would spot them. The dark night hid them well, and they became invisible for all to see. They walked towards the bend in the road, a bend they had walked around one million times before, but this time walking around the bend meant so much more to them. Arty Grape felt it might be the last time she would ever see her home again. They had reached the point of no return, and walking past this point meant they could no longer see their house. She knew once she had passed it there would be no going back. She stopped and she looked behind her.

Mr Fox hadn't noticed his sister stopping, so he kept walking until he realised. 'Arty! What are you doing? Are we going to keep walking?'

'Yes, I was just thinking for a moment,' she said. Arty Grape was thinking about turning around. She was thinking about going home and climbing back into her warm bed, but Mr Fox's unwavering will gave her the courage to carry on. She reached for his hand and they walked side by side before stopping at the gate that she had hoped to find. It was a wooden gate that guarded the baron grasslands where the horses used to roam free.

'We're going in there?' asked Mr Fox.

'Yeah, I'll go first.' Arty Grape stepped up to the gate and climbed over. It was easy to climb, it was like a step ladder, all you needed to do was to put one foot above the other and swing your body over the top. Mr Fox followed with ease and they settled themselves a little before they continued. Arty Grape was scared and anxious and she felt scared and anxious for her brother too – she was the one that had brought him here and she felt responsible for every one of his moves. 'You okay Fox?' she asked. 'Do you want to go back?'

'No. I'm okay. I'm a bit cold, but I'm okay. Do you know where you're going?'

'Of course I do,' she said, but Arty Grape only hoped she did. 'We'll head that way, there's a path that's hidden, ahead. I remember being told about it years ago.'

They carried on walking through the uneven field. The untended grass grabbed at their knees as they walked and they both wondered if what they were doing was a good idea. It was dark, it was cold, it was scary, and they could hardly see each step that they took.

Not many people would choose to do what they were doing at that time of the day – you would be a complete fool if you did. All manner of things wait in the shadows at that time of day. They wait for any opportunity to snatch you away and do unspeakable things to you.

Every step meant the light that existed began to fade. It left them slowly. It became darker and darker and more weird too, just like this story I hope.

'You're weird.'

'Why thank you, kind sir.'

Arty Grape kept walking and kept looking for any opening at the edge of the field. She was sure it was there, and she was sure her papa had wanted her to know it was there. They reached the part of the field where the trees began, and she continued to look for the elusive opening. 'This way Fox,' she said, and Mr Fox followed.

They worked their way along the edge of the trees, far into the field. Mr Fox looked back and he couldn't figure out where the gate he had climbed was. He stayed as close as he could to his sister. He didn't want her to disappear from his sight, and he didn't want to be left alone.

'Ah, here it is. I knew it was here somewhere.' Arty Grape had found the opening and it was where her world ended and mine begins. Nothing would be the same after they stepped into that gap in the trees: the woods and the tower would now own them.

They pulled some heavy branches aside and stepped through the trees. They found a path on the other side, which immediately became more difficult to follow. It began to work its way down into a forest that they had forgotten was there. It weaved and it wound itself downwards. Loose stones would slide under their feet, and while a slight misstep at this point in the story wouldn't have mattered, it still would have hurt. They carefully stepped along the path. To their side lay a small gully of nettles and branches that hid a pool of stagnant and disgusting water. The path didn't care about you and it would punish you for any mistake that was made. It would laugh hard should you stumble – just like the devil would laugh at you when that moment arrived: the moment when you realised your parents had already sold your soul to him the very instant you were born.

Down and down they went, following the path that had ensnared them. The sounds of the river became more noticeable. It had always been there, but the tranquil sound had managed to fill their heads without them realising. Their minds had been pre-occupied with the task of not dying, not falling over and not hitting their heads on the inviting death rocks that surrounded them. They slid carefully down to the bottom of the path and found themselves a river, whose ice-cold waters flowed. They had overcome the first part of their journey and for a brief moment they didn't have a care in the world. They were happy, even though they had such a long way to go. They sat down on the ground and they listened to the musical majesty of the river flowing past them. They were completely unaware that the path was about to become even more of a-- I'll leave that last word to your imagination.

'Let's carry on now. We're nearly there,' Arty Grape said.

Arty Grape and Mr Fox weren't *nearly there*, they were as far from *there* as *there* could be, but I wasn't going to tell them that.

Life is so short, questionable and evanescent that it is not worth the trouble of major effort.

Wondering The Wilderness

As they continued to walk cautiously in the pale moonlight, through the dense trees, there was a certain silence in the air. Only the wondrous stars in the sky made any kind of noise. Arty Grape and Mr Fox could hear their own footsteps, but soon even those became invisible to them. Mr Fox was following Arty Grape. He had no idea where he was going or what was coming next. He had never been there before and he didn't think his sister had been there either – he could tell this by the fear he saw in her eyes when she looked at him to reassure him that everything was okay. 'It's not okay Fox, it's not okay,' was what her eyes told him.

The trees swooped over them like guardian angels from above. It was pitch black, but you could still see the green of the leaves glowing, courtesy of the brilliant moon. The tree roots grew from out of the ground, and each felt like an ancient warrior that had survived through the ages. The trees had been there for hundreds of years. Some had fallen and some would stand proud for another hundred years... or they could fall at any moment crushing the children beneath them. The trees grew tall, the leaves were a deep green and they carefully hid you from the light. It was a dark forest that glowed. If you could see the forest in the light of day you would wander at its wonder.

As they navigated the path, the sounds they heard became more peculiar and the path felt more strange. The sound of the water had taken over everything. Like a travelling spirit, the water always had somewhere to go, but it never worried about getting there.

'Arty,' whispered Mr Fox. Why he whispered nobody knew, not even God could hear them now--if you believe in him.

'What?' she whispered back. She knew exactly what he was going to say even moments before he had thought it.

'You always get wet near water.'

Arty Grape did always get wet near water, it was as inevitable as a self-fulfilling prophecy. 'Let's just keep following the path, it has to take us somewhere that we need to go.'

Mr Fox didn't say anything. He had followed Arty Grape this far and he thought he may as well keep following her.

The path kept winding, disappearing up and then down. It had become a conveyer belt that took them wherever it pleased, they were at its mercy.

They walked for some time and they only stopped to stare at a beautiful waterfall along the way. They heard the sound of the water change, so they peered over the path. They watched and they listened to the water tumbling over the waterfall's edge, every drop crashing like thunder onto the rocks beneath it. They carried on walking moments before the sound of the waterfall overcame them. The path didn't make things easy, there were so many obstacles in their way. They had to jump over things, go through things and step over boggy patches but, no matter what, the path never left them and they always found their way to being lost. They had passed many things and many opportunities to die should their feet slip slightly from underneath them. Their breathing became heavy as the path started to climb in front of them, and a two-hundred-foot drop kept them company at their side. It would have been a messy death if they were to fall. Somebody would have to find and identify their bodies, which is something nobody wants to do.

The path suddenly came to an end, they had followed it like the walking dead and when it ended they didn't know what to do, until they looked up. The path did continue but it was on the other side of the wide and unforgiving river.

'We have to get across the river,' Arty Grape said confidently. She had absolutely no idea what she was doing, so please don't think that she did. Just like most of us she just put one foot in front of the other.

Inconveniently placed rocks connected the two distant sides, each rock more dangerously placed than the last. These rocks had to be conquered because Arty Grape and Mr Fox were not to be stopped; they were *not* to be stopped. Arty Grape turned to Mr Fox: 'We have to cross the river, can you do it? If you can't then I have to leave you here, you have to go back the way you came. Can you do it?'

'You're not leaving me and I'm not leaving you. I can do it.'

'Okay. Let's do it then. I'll go first.' Arty Grape took several long and deep breaths before attacking the rocks and doing battle with the river. There stood six rocks in front of her, each with a stoic look on its face, a face that taunted you, a face you wanted to punch. In her head she could hear the music from the movie *Chariots of Fire* – and when the time was right and the music hit the note she was waiting for, she bolted towards her possible doom... which we shall call *Possabilladoom*. She moved like angel that swept down to the earth to free its people of their misery. Her legs moved like she was a dancer on a stage; every move was gracefully executed, of course it was, we *are* talking about Arty Grape here. She continued to leap across the rocks, bouncing from one to the other without hesitation, it was as if the air was guiding her to the other side. A thought of her brother popped into her head briefly and it distracted her. She lost all her momentum and stopped. She steadied herself on the rock before looking up to find two more rocks sitting between her and the riverbank. The rocks looked steady, but from her experience rocks always looked steady until you stepped on them – only then do you find out that they will wobble like a crazy fool. Arty Grape mentally prepared herself to perform two jumps in one swift movement, if you get my meaning (and if that is actually possible?). 'Easy-peasy, lemon Gaaahwyjiiibaaaaaaaah!' she whispered to herself, before taking her final leap of faith across the slippery stones. To her surprise, as much as to anyone reading this, Arty Grape had finished up just where she intended to be! She was back on dry land, it wasn't a myth. Her brain was attempting to catch up with the actions that her body had performed. She had no memory of the events that had occurred only moments ago. Those events had been changed and they had been altered, she would forever remember them differently. She had been left with only the feeling of how her body had moved. She closed her eyes and composed herself again. Even though she didn't believe in the gods, she still thanked one of them anyway. Then she turned to Mr Fox, it was his turn now and there was no telling how that was going to end. *Maybe I should have let him go first and instructed him across* she thought, but what did it matter? It would be the exact same situation, just in reverse. *At least he saw me do it* she thought.

'Are you okay?' shouted Mr Fox.

'I'm fine, it's easy; you'll be fine.'

I'm sure even you don't believe that. Of course it wasn't easy, it was bloody ridiculously hard and a stupid thing to do. Arty Grape was lying to him and to herself – she didn't know if everything was going to be okay, nobody ever does. At least it was a good lie. Sometimes lies can be good, you know – why would they exist if they weren't like beautiful mistakes waiting to happen?

She didn't want to worry Mr Fox any more than was necessary, who wants to know that the thing they are about to do is as treacherous as treacherous can be? 'Don't worry take your time. You'll be fine.' Those dreaded five words – *You'll be fine.*

Mr Fox stood silently and analysed the rocks. He thought about the slippage factor and the distance of each of them. He thought about how his stride would have to change from one leap to the next. 'Arty, count to three and then I'm going.'

'Are you sure?'

'Yes, count to three.'

'Okay. One elephant, two elephants, three elephants.'

On the third elephant Mr Fox sprang into action. The rocks became mere stepping stones in his story, taking him from page to page. He looked like an Olympic athlete with every stride, gliding across the slippery surfaces with ease... But alas he didn't make it to the other side, but you knew that didn't you? Everything happened in slow motion, of course. Until that is, it didn't – and then it did again. The legs of Mr Fox flew from underneath his body and his arms flayed in the air, and his life, even though short, flashed in front of his eyes. He was helpless, suspended in the air with only one way to go – up.

Arty Grape didn't know what to do. Her whole body froze until Mr Fox hit the water with an almighty crash. Thank goodness Mr Fox had fallen into the water between the rocks, otherwise he would have been dead in an instant, his head and body smashed into little pieces.

A humongous splash rocketed through the air and at the peak of the splash you could hear the sound of the water laughing. Oooooh, how the water laughed at Mr Fox. They were naive to think that they would both escape before getting to hear the roar of its cruel laugh. 'I've got you now, you are mine,' it said. The hands of the water reached around Mr Fox's body and dragged him down, he had no choice but to go to where the water was taking him. He was buried beneath the face of the river, and he was gone, but not forever. Seconds felt like minutes, minutes felt like hours, and days felt like daisies. Eventually the water began to calm, and only ripples remained to mark the spot where Mr Fox had fallen in.

Arty Grape was still frozen, staring at the water that had taken her brother prisoner. She couldn't believe what had happened. *Is this it? Will I ever see my brother again* she thought. She had had these thoughts before, but she never thought they would become real, and so soon. This couldn't be the last moment that she would see her brother again! There was no way she was going to allow that to happen! Surely she had to have some control over it? She began to will him out of the water with all her might. Her thoughts turned into an immense power and she willed and she willed, without ever turning to prayer. Arty Grape had no time for prayer.

Still Wondering

Why did Arty Grape have no time for prayer? Well, she had never heard of any scientific proof that prayer had ever worked, so she decided not to waste another moment on it. I suppose that kind of thing can never be scientific anyway, or ever proved. One just has to have faith, and we all know faith trumps all. I could ramble on but I won't, I'll stop myself this time. See, I can do it.

If I continue to ramble I might forget about dear Mr Fox who is still buried deep within the icy waters. He must be wondering what he's doing there and why I'm keeping him down there for an unnecessary amount of time. Why am I drowning the life out of him? What did he do to deserve this cold death? I hadn't decided what I would do with Mr Fox for a very long time and then it came to me: What kind of sick and twisted woman would I be if I killed off one of my own creations? What repercussions would it have in this world of mine? So there we have it. Mr Fox will live to see another packet of sweets. He'll be back very soon but until then you are stuck with me. I'm going to take you wherever I want you to go, this journey of mine isn't over yet.

Mr Fox burst out of the water in the same manner he had fallen into it. He was cold, he was freaked out and frankly he was annoyed by everything that had just happened. He spluttered and then he gasped, and water poured out of him wherever it was possible. The ice cold water was enough of a terrible experience, but nearly drowning in it was unnecessary, it would have been the worst possible way to exit to the left.

'I thought I'd lost you!' screamed Arty Grape. She, like Mr Fox, was breathing for the very first time again. She jumped towards him, completely forgetting about her own safety. She stumbled and then fell onto the rock nearest her brother. 'Reach out and give me your hand, I'll pull you out.' She stretched her body as much as she could so he could grab her hand. Mr Fox stretched his hand as much as he could too. They only had one chance at getting this right, there wasn't room for error. They locked their hands together, and immediately Arty Grape pulled as hard she could... but nothing happened. Mr Fox held on tight and Arty Grape pulled and pulled ten times more. It was only on the eleventh time she realised that Mr Fox's foot was lodged under something neither of them could see. Arty Grape tried to pull him again but he didn't move, not even ever so slightly. She was getting tired but she had no choice other than to carry on – he couldn't stay there and she couldn't leave him there either. 'Okay! Let's try again,' she said, exhaustedly. Arty Grape felt a surge of energy travel from her mind and through her body to her weakening arms, and she pulled her brother again. She felt her heave resonate through her body into Mr Fox's body, and they combined both theirs *wills*, so it equalled *will x 2*.

To each of their surprise he was set free, or as free as we can ever think we are. The one thing led her to another thing, something they both weren't expecting: the gap between Arty Grape and Mr Fox began to widen unexpectedly! It seemed what had kept him stuck had also kept him from drifting away. As the current started carrying Mr Fox off Arty Grape could no longer hold on to him, he was too heavy and the current was too strong. He slowly drifted away from her and their fingers eventually parted.

'Arty...Heeeeeeeelp!' screamed Mr Fox. 'Heeeeeelp!'

'Hold on Fox! Hold on!'

Mr Fox was heading towards another beautiful waterfall along the path. It wasn't a large waterfall and it didn't look beautiful to Mr Fox anymore, and anyone falling over it would not live to tell any more tales. At its watery feet were more ancient rocks – how many lives they had claimed had never been spoken.

Arty Grape did the only thing she could think of, she clambered off the rocks and back onto the riverbank as quickly as she could, nearly meeting her watery doom along the way. She saw a path at the top of the riverbank and climbed towards it. The wet mud slid under her feet, preventing her reaching the top as quickly as she would have liked. Mr Fox was still drifting towards the waterfall and Arty Grape's only hope was to get there before he did. She ran down the path and anticipated where Mr Fox would flow. She hurried through the trees, keeping one eye ahead of her and one eye on her brother. If her calculations were correct, she knew the exact spot that he was heading for and she ran towards it with great determination, nothing could stand in her way. She ran as fast as she could and leapt over anything that tried to interfere with her task; she was a machine after all. In the distance she saw an opening in the trees leading back down to the river. She couldn't risk not taking it, she couldn't risk there not being another opening further along the path, so she took her chance. Once again she found herself running towards the water, when she had hoped that she would never have to meddle with its dark powers again. She spotted a large flat rock sitting in the water and waited until she was close enough before she threw her body onto it. It was wet and covered in green moss, so she slid for a little and came to a stop with half her body hanging over its edge. She shimmied back, she didn't want to be pulled into the water by Mr Fox, so she dug her feet between two rocks behind her. She looked to see where Mr Fox was. He would soon float past her, he was travelling fast and panicking as the water took him against his will. Arty Grape lunged and she plunged as much as she could, stretching her presence as much as she could. 'Fox!' she shouted. 'Try and swim towards me. Grab my hand.' This was the only chance she had. It looked as though certain death was a promise that had already been rolled with Mr Fox's dice. Her hand reached for him, her fingers shot out like arrows. Mr Fox tried to swim as hard as he could, splashing in the water like his dear life depended on it. He edged, slowly but surely, towards his sister and he threw out his hand, kicking his legs like crazy. 'Grab on to me! Grab my hand and don't let go!' Arty Grape shouted. He sped towards her and his fingers brushed hers. Arty Grape had to stretch her body even more, her feet and her body dug even more into the rocks behind her. 'Aaaaaaaaaaaggggghhhhhhh!' she screamed, before grabbing his hand hard. They grabbed each other so hard and so tight, you couldn't tell who was rescuing who. The speed at which Mr Fox was travelling nearly pulled Arty Grape into the water, but she held on until he was steady. Her muscles burned and it took all her emotional and physical strength not to let go. Mr Fox was still being dragged away from his sister, but Arty Grape wasn't about to let go. She looked at him, directly in his eyes. He could tell from her gaze alone that she wasn't going to let him go. Arty Grape pulled once again with all her might, and added just a little bit more. They both made sure that each other were okay during this terrible ordeal that neither would like to re-live.

Arty Grape slowly and carefully dragged her brother to the

riverbank. 'Hold on tight Fox, I'll pull you in, don't let go. I'll pull you towards the bank over there.' She reached her other arm out and wrapped it around his wrist and began to pull him in. There was no delicacy involved in the situation, her grip burned into his skin and the bones in their fingers felt like they were being ground down by each other as she slowly freed him from the current.

Once he was behind the flat rock, things became easier and he climbed up the muddy riverbank until he was out of danger. Arty Grape joined him at his side. They both lay back on the hard ground, they were exhausted and they wondered what was coming next. They listened to each other breathing hard, struggling to take normal breaths.

The tower on the hill wasn't going to make things easy for them, they knew that now, they had been fools to think otherwise. The tower is only for those worthy enough to enter. What things will they see along the way? What things will they learn? What mistakes will they make? Their journey is only just beginning and reaching the tower on the hill is just one insignificant part of it.

This Is The The End

Arty Grape thought they had reached the end of their journey. There was no other way to go but home... but going home meant getting across the river again and the river wasn't going to let them pass.

'We're not going back, I hate going backwards,' said Mr Fox, he could see what his sister was thinking by the look on her face, it *always* gave everything away.

'You hate going backwards. What does that even mean?' she barked back.

'Yes. You know, travelling in reverse, where the future is the past.'

'Travelling in reverse? What does that even mean?'

'I just don't like going backwards.'

'Okay. We won't go backwards then. Are you sure?'

'I'm sure.' Mr Fox was cold but luckily it wasn't the winter months, otherwise he would have frozen, instead he would eventually dry.

They slowly made their way back to the path, it felt like Arty Grape had to drag him there, he was a broken young man, he had never faced death before and he didn't want to face it again for a long time. They stepped carefully over the rocks until they found a dry spot to sit on to rest for a minute or two. Up ahead the path looked less friendly again, it slowly meandered up the hill and then it disappeared over its brow.

'So shall we continue then?' asked Arty Grape.

'Let me sit for a minute, I'm so tired and I just nearly died.'

Arty Grape was tired too, they had risen early and she hadn't had the twelve hours of sleep that she had become accustomed too. Mr Fox started to shiver slightly next to her, so she took her coat off, wrapped it around him, held him close and shared her warmth with him.

'Okay. It won't be long. We'll be there soon. If you want to go back, I'll come with you. We'll try and find a better way back across the river.' said Arty Grape.

'We're not going back. Let's just keep going.'

They looked around and realised the path now veered in two directions. Up until that moment they had just followed it in one direction, they never thought they would have to make a choice. They now had two different directions that they could travel and a small dilemma.

Mr Fox stood up. He was ready to tackle whatever lay ahead. 'Let's do it then!' he said with gusto.

'Okay, let's do it,' replied Arty Grape enthusiastically. They were putting themselves into a new state of mind. They switched into a new mode--*Click*.

Arty Grape looked at both parts of the path. She would choose the way they would continue, and she eventually decided that they would keep moving in the same direction as they had come. They weren't going backwards, they were going forwards. The path wasn't going to trick them and they weren't going to let it bother them anymore.

They set off and continued their journey to the tower on the hill. They walked up the natural steps that had been carved into the land by the rising tree roots. The tree roots had refused to be tread down by all the other travellers that once passed. Arty Grape and Mr Fox continued to climb the mountain, and with every small footstep it became steeper. It was overgrown in some parts, and in other parts the path would mysteriously disappear only to reappear several steps later. Why did Arty Grape assume that the path would always be there? Don't we all lose our way sometimes?

Everything in front of them continued to wind, and the tree roots forced their way through the earth harder than before. They kept climbing without speaking. They just listened to the trees and the water talk to each other, just like they had done before. They were in the forest's domain now. As they climbed the sound of the water became fainter, but it had been engraved into their minds and it remained with them long after it had gone. They could no longer see the moon through the branches of the trees above. The trees had encased them in a dark tomb and stared down at them, watching their every move. They walked and walked, and their little bodies became tired. It seemed that there was no end to this uphill struggle. Further and further they walked into the dark wood, holding each other close.

'What was that?' Arty Grape shouted and whispered.

'What?'

'I heard something – it sounded like a branch snapping. Somebody's there.'

They stopped and looked deep into the forest. They couldn't see anything but Arty Grape was sure somebody else was there.

'Maybe it's a fox or a badger or a...' Mr Fox was trying to convince himself that it was anything other than somebody following them through the night. 'I can't see anything. There's nothing there, Arty. Stop freaking me out.'

If there was something or somebody there, it didn't want to be seen.

Their legs ached and their feet throbbed. The path was beating them down bit by bit. When they thought they could walk no further, they saw an opening in the endless trees and they thought they could see the glimmer of the clouds in the sky. Arty Grape didn't know if it was a welcome sight or not. It made her feel nervous because she didn't know what was coming next, and what or who they would meet. Arty Grape knew *nothing*. They were following each other and they were following something greater than themselves.

The trees began to open up and the light from above slowly entered.

'Look, Fox. There's an opening up ahead. Maybe that's it. Maybe we've reached the tower.'

'Is that where we're going? I hope it's there. I'm so tired. I don't know how much longer I can keep going,' he moaned.

'Me too. We're nearly there. I wonder how we'll get in? I wonder if there's a door? I wonder if there's a doorbell?' Arty Grape hadn't even thought about how she would get into the tower on the hill, her only thoughts had been getting there-- One thing at a time, I suppose.

Arty Grape had her eyes fixed on the opening and on the arrival of the new light. They still had a little way to go before they reached it. Mr Fox was looking up and looking down, and then he looked across and over there. Whilst Arty Grape's eyes were fixated on the opening, his eyes were on something he never thought he would see... It was the NoWhereMan.

The NoWhereMan was standing there as if he was a normal sight to see. He didn't make a single move. He was standing with his back to them. He began to slowly take off his hooded jacket; finally Mr Fox thought he would see his face for the first time. Maybe he was someone they knew after all this time, pretending to be someone and something else?

'Arty!' Mr Fox whispered as they continued to walk.

'What?' she whispered back, her eyes still fixed on the light.

'Look. Look over there.'

Arty Grape stopped walking and turned to where her brother was pointing. It *was* the NoWhereMan and he was just standing there, Mr Fox hadn't imagined it. Arty Grape was surprised too, and even she didn't know what he was doing. They just waited, staring at him in disbelief.

'Shall we say something?' asked Mr Fox.

'I don't know. Maybe we should, maybe he can help us?'

Arty Grape was about to call out to the NoWhereMan. As her lips pursed to form the sounds, the NoWhereMan ran into the arms of the forest with great speed. It was like someone had fired a starter pistol and he was running the race of his life. They watched him run through the trees until he disappeared from sight. Soon they couldn't see him but they could hear him rustling through the trees as he moved.

'What was that?' Mr Fox puzzled.

'I have no idea. That was just weird, that's what *that* was!'

'What's he doing here? Is he following us? Has he always been following us, has he always been there?'

Neither Arty Grape nor Mr Fox had any answers, so there was only one thing that they could do. They carried on. The NoWhereMan was in the forest just like them, and maybe he too was travelling to the tower on the hill. Or maybe he was travelling back to where he had come from.

The NoWhereMan had strangely made Mr Fox feel safe and comfortable. For some reason seeing him had helped Mr Fox feel that nothing bad was going to happen--no matter how bad you think that happen is going to be.

Nearly There

The forest became thinner and thinner and the light started to bounce off and through the trees. The sun was beginning to rise slowly and they began to remember that they had forgotten about the light, but there it was, and the darkness slowly lifted. The darkness scares most people because strange things go on in the night, if you're lucky enough to see them.

Arty Grape and Mr Fox made their way through the remaining trees. They didn't run into the arms of the light, they dragged their bodies slowly towards it like the living dead. The sunrise was a pure vision – it captured their attention and the forest behind them was a distant memory – they gazed at its glorious sight. The sunrise is a beautiful thing to witness. It's a time when most people are asleep, just like you are sleeping right now, comfortable in your bed, and dreaming of things you would never dare tell other people. Those horrific thoughts that will never be known, unless you speak of them. One day someone will come for your thoughts too, where will you hide then?

Arty Grape and Mr Fox both returned from one of the many trances they would experience throughout their lives. The sunrise in all its beauty had held them hostage long enough. It was time to continue. In front of them, but a little bit to the side, stood a LitteGirl with very pale skin wearing an extremely severe haircut. It looked like somebody had used some elaborate tool to cut it at right angles to itself. The LitteGirl's hair reached down to her black eyebrows where her eyes began – eyes usually begin around about there. Her deep dark eyes were as deep as they were dark. When your gaze finally reached her mouth you were greeted by the loveliest of smiles and perfect bright white teeth. The LitteGirl stood like a soldier, she didn't move or hesitate to move. It was a strange yet comfortable moment that they all shared. She slowly raised her arm and pointed in one direction, and turned her head to look in another, grinning through all these individual moments. The LitteGirl soon returned to her former stance and then she faded away. She was no more and she would never appear in this story again, she had served her purpose as their strange and confusing guide.

Arty Grape looked at Mr Fox and Mr Fox looked at Arty Grape. 'I guess we should go that way then,' said Arty Grape, ignoring the fact that a little girl had just disappeared in front of them.

'Of course we should,' said Mr Fox.

They headed *that* way, towards a grassy path. I don't know about you but I've not been led down the wrong path yet. That reminds me of an ancient saying (when I say 'reminds me' I mean I just looked it up), it said the *road less travelled* but the actual saying is *the road not taken*. Arty Grape decided to take the road not taken and let it lead her to wherever it wanted to. The path looked warm and it looked inviting. It wound around the mountain they thought they had finished climbing, it swayed up and down small hills and disappeared around corners. They had stopped guessing what was around each corner a long time ago. They held each other's hand and carried on, never giving up, plodding forwards with a huge amount of hope in their hearts. Hope was the only thing that they had left; they had to tell themselves that everything would be okay in the end.

Arty Grape and Mr Fox followed the landscape blindly, and it soon became plain and boring as well as uphill all the way. The only colours they saw were green, grey and blue. The only objects were the sunshine and the carcasses of dead animals, the rotting corpses of what once was: the bones of goats and sheep, a jawbone or an entire head stripped of all its worldly flesh. This was the first time Arty Grape and Mr Fox had seen such things and they didn't know if the bones and bodies of these animals were some kind of sign of what lay ahead. They held each other even closer without even knowing they were doing it. Their breathing became heavier and heavier with every carefully placed step.

'Let's stop for a minute,' wheezed Mr Fox. 'Let's sit on that rock over there.'

Arty Grape was more than happy to sit for a little while, too. Even if the rock looked cold and hard, to Arty Grape it looked like the most comfortable seat in the world. They wheezed their way towads the rock and sat down, they had no real idea of how long they had been walking or how far they had ascended. They rested their tiny feet and took a moment to themselves. They could see the town of Eden very clearly below. They were looking at it from up on high. They had climbed higher than they had ever imagined, the entire town sat beneath them. They had never seen the entire town all at once like that before. From a distance it looked like a ghost town, abandoned and without life.

Maybe it is a ghost town? Arty Grape thought. 'Look Fox, look over there, you can see our house. I can see the back of it creeping out through those trees down there. Do you see it?' Mr Fox stared for some time and tried to figure out where his sister was pointing. Arty Grape knew where she was pointing, but it's pretty much nearly impossible for the other person to know – that is without doing some kind of complicated trigonometry calculation.

'Where?' asked Mr Fox.

'Over there.'

'There?' he questioned again.

'No! There... Right where I'm pointing...There!'

'What, there?'

'No! There! There! Oooh never mind.'

A short silence followed before Arty Grape spoke again. 'I wonder what Mama and Papa are doing right now? Pretending to be asleep I bet, just in case we come in.'

'I hope they are asleep,' said Mr Fox. 'Otherwise they'll eventually find out we're not there.'

Arty Grape and Mr Fox weren't *there* and they wouldn't be going back *there* for a very long time. The tower of the hill would become their home for a while, when they finally reached it, because they did reach it and they did find their way inside, of course they did. What they will find inside even eludes me right now. First I have to pad these pages out with endless words and descriptions hoping that along the way you don't get too bored. It doesn't matter if I make sense to you or not, I don't make sense to a lot of people.

'Let's rock,' Arty Grape enthusiastically shouted, springing to her feet as she said it.

'Let's rock,' Mr Fox said, springing to his feet less enthusiastically.

Arty slowly climbed off the rock and looked for the path again. It had started to slowly disappear back into the mountain for some time now, and the more they tried to follow it the more it left them. They were making their own path and following their own way. Arty Grape felt privileged, with each step she felt she was carving a new piece into the world.

They held each other's hand and they climbed. The wild grass became thicker and longer, it became even more of a struggle to move forward. The long grass felt like it was pushing them back, warning them or trying to keep them away. The breeze in the air made the grass whisper and, at paranoid times, it sounded like it was talking to Arty Grape in all manner of different voices. *Where are you gooooooooooing? Loooooooooook ooooooooover theeeeeeeeeeeeere. Keeeeeeeeeeeep goooooooooooooing. Go baaaaaack.* Arty Grape was able to ignore the voices in her head, she had been blocking them out for many years, but the grass spoke in a different voice and it was harder to ignore.

Mr Fox hadn't started to hear the voices in his head yet, but who knew if that day would come? Most people escape the affliction of these disturbing things.

They were both exhausted, their heads had dropped and they were staring at the ground as they walked. When they finally did manage to look up they saw the tower of the hill in the distance, it had snuck up on them despite its size. It cast a huge shadow across the land and it seemed to suck the surrounding clouds towards it like it exuded its own gravity.

'Look Fox! The tower!'

'I see it, Arty. It's huge.'

'It is, isn't it? I didn't think it was that big, it looks so small when you look at it from Eden.' The tower stretched across the land. From the town it looked tall but it was as tall as it was wide, dominating everything around it. 'We're nearly there and we're not going back.'

After seeing the tower they both had a renewed energy, their heads lifted up, their shoulders went back, and they kept the tower in their sights. The tower became bigger and bigger and its force stronger and stronger with every stride they took, until it was right in front of them, looking wise with all its age. It didn't blink and it didn't apologise for its overbearing presence, it sat tall and proud. Its structure towered over them, reaching far into the sky.

They gazed at it for a little longer, before they noticed something out of the corner of their eyes... In the distance, a tall thin man worked his way from behind the tower and slowly walked towards them, moving forwards and backwards at the same time. They waited and waited. The tall thin man was taking forever to reach them. *Hurry up man! Get there already!* I'm thinking. The more he approached, the more his features could be distinguished. He wore all black and he had a light hood over his head that was part of his all-in-one get-up. The tall man had a neutral look on his aged face. His eyes were the strangest of things that Arty Grape and Mr Fox had ever seen, it looked like he could see behind himself. To him the future *was* the past. The tall thin man stopped and stooped over them... and then the sound of one thousand horns filled the air, it almost blew Arty Grape and Mr Fox off their feet. The pleasurable tones of the horn soothed them to begin with, but then they started to become painful, the sound waves began to pierce their eardrums. 'A A A A A A A R R R R R R T T T T T T Y Y Y Y Y GRRRRRAAAAAAAAAAAAPE!!!!!' she shouted, and up until this very day she doesn't know why she shouted out her own name. Her body began to convulse and she couldn't make it stop until the strange-eyed man looked at her hard and very carefully.

'Welcome. You are most welcome,' he smirked.

A door began to form and open in the walls of the tower. As it opened it made a loud noise, it was like the door of Aladdin's cave being rolled to one side – you know, the sound of stone being dragged across stone.

Shall we leave it there for now? Shall we continue with the next chapter? Personally, I think before I begin again, making up these facts, I'm going to need some supplementary restraint.

The Looming Tower

The door in the tower on the hill took forever to open, it was a stupid amount of time, and whilst it was opening Arty Grape continued to stare at the strange-eyed man; the strange-eyed man looked at Mr Fox; and Mr Fox looked at the door opening. None were the wiser.

Finally the door was fully open and if they were allowed, they would enter. The man with the strange eyes looked at them for the last time before turning and walking to the opening. 'Follow me please,' he said, before walking through the door in the tower, to never be seen again. People keep disappearing in this story, I wonder if Arty Grape or Mr Fox will disappear too? Just like I did that very day.

This was the moment that they had come here for, they just didn't think getting in would be so easy. They were welcomed as if they were expected. Arty Grape had thought that they would have to fight or figure out how to get in, not be welcomed in by a strange man. She gazed into the darkness behind the door, Mr Fox was lost in its mystery too. They stepped forward, and with that first step Arty Grape began to hear the voices. They were the same voices that had called her to the tower, and the voices she had always pretended not to hear, they had become louder in her head. They could sense her hesitation, so the voices persuaded her in whispers that everything would be okay.

'Come on Arty, what are we waiting for?' Mr Fox didn't seem hesitant at all, he was strangely eager to see what delights were waiting for him. He pulled his sister with him and for the first time, Arty Grape was following him. She wasn't making the choices anymore and she wondered if she ever had been.

They slowly eased their way across the threshold of the exit of their minds. They were now where they wanted to be, it would become their home for the many seconds of time. The door didn't slam behind them like you might expect it to; it remained open for all eternity. It would become one of the many doors that would always remain open.

They both turned to look at the forest, wondering if they should go back the way they came, but it was too late, there was nothing behind them anymore. The forest had gone, the door had gone, everything had gone. Arty Grape and Mr Fox were in a vacuum, and nothing else existed but them. They turned around again but they couldn't be sure if they were facing the same direction they were a moment ago, it had become too dark to know. They floated forwards into nothing, they were careful not to let each other go. A surge of electricity sounded and they felt the frequency of the sound resonate through their bodies, their bones nearly exploded from their skin. A door in the distance became illuminated by a soft pink light, and the closer they floated towards the door the more other doors began to appear to them, each illuminated by a different coloured light. Their hearts pounded hard, every beat could be felt and heard and every beat pushed them further forwards. They looked up into the expanse above and they could see the stars in the night sky. The stars were so close they could nearly touch them. They could see all the constellations forming, and they could see a part of the magical Milky Way. The universe was vast and they realised they were only a tiny part of it. Planets orbited around the sun; stars burst into supernova; black holes devoured light and dark matter without a care in the world.

The doors continued to form in front of them and they started to feel the floor beneath their feet. They were getting closer and closer, and the stars and planets moved further away. They moved closer to the door that had first become illuminated. It was a large and solid-looking wooden door. The door was blocking their way forward, they dared not move further into the darkness that surrounded it. Scrawled on the door's face were words that had faded, but you could still decipher them--*Thoughtfulness.*

'What do we do now Arty? What do we do next Arty?' Mr Fox asked anxiously. 'Do we go through this door? Do we go to the other doors?'

'Let's see what the other doors say.' Arty Grape remained calm. She had to remain calm to keep her brother calm, but really she was like a duck paddling in still waters.

'Okay, this way or that way?' asked Mr Fox.

'It's always this way, Fox. You should know that by now.'

They moved towards one of the other doors, investigating what words, if any, were written on them. One by one they walked to each door. How many doors there were, they didn't know, they had lost count and they spread in both directions.

Reason,   Honesty,   Trust,   Love,   Integrity,   Compassion, Happiness, Discipline, Respect echoed the doors.

They didn't think to open any of the them, they were only interested in what the doors had to say to them, without speaking.

Arty Grape moved towards the next door. There were no words written on it. 'I don't know why Fox, but I want to go through this door,' she said, but Mr Fox didn't answer. 'Fox! Shall we open this door? Fox! What do you think?'

Mr Fox was no longer with her, he had parted from her side. Mr Fox was stood at another door, and what that door said Arty Grape didn't know. Her heart sank as she watched him walk forward through it, and then he was gone. Mr Fox had opened and walked through his own door, it mattered not that Arty Grape didn't know which door it was. Mr Fox was on his own journey now and Arty Grape was on hers. She didn't feel worried about her brother, she knew he would be okay, so she decided to walk through her door. And then she was gone too. The tower had taken her.

Where Am I? Who Am I?

The White Room

You may have read this far but I'm not so sure I'll be able to keep you for much longer. This is the point in the story where things start to get strange. The world is strange so I decided to right down all the strangeness that *I* can see. I don't blame you if you put the book down – but if you do then you will *never* find out what happens to Arty Grape and Mr Fox. Do you care? Do I care?

Arty Grape found herself in another dark room, void of anything else but the absence of colour. Before materialising in the room, she had already travelled through many places and across many times. Sometimes when you open a door there is a surprise waiting behind it – sometimes pleasant and sometime un-pleasant.

She took a few careful steps forward and the darkness changed to a blinding white light, like God had just turned the lights on. Her eyes failed her for a few moments, it felt like forever, but her blindness soon passed, leaving her with blurred vision. A silhouetted figure skipped towards her. Arty Grape imagined the silhouette to be an elegant lady, so the shadowy figure became an elegant lady, and she skipped towards her until their noses touched. They stood nose to nose for exactly one minute. They didn't say a word to each other in this time, they just looked into each other's eyes. It couldn't have been easy for the elegant lady because she was taller than Arty Grape, so she had to squat a little to reach Arty Grape's level. Arty Grape weirdly thought that she must have strong legs to hold that position for that amount of time. All manner of strange things popped into Arty Grape's head, sometimes at the most inconvenient moments.

Arty Grape knew exactly one minute had passed because the elegant lady had held a stopwatch in front of her face, pressed a button, and then pressed the button again exactly one minute later to stop it. After the time had expired, the lady moonwalked backwards, creating a reasonable amount of personal space between the two of them.

Moonwalking backwards didn't appear strange to Arty Grape, it had always seemed like a fun way to travel and her papa had attempted to do it many times, but he had always failed, quite badly. *Mama and Papa*, Arty Grape thought. Arty Grape suddenly missed them and she wanted to see them again; she wanted to be held by them and be told that everything was okay, but instead she was in the tower on the hill, in the place she always wanted to be.

Finally her vision restored back to normal and she could clearly see the elegant lady's face, and she could feel that the elegant lady was warm and friendly. That put Arty Grape very much at ease. The elegant lady was smartly dressed. She was a cool casual lady, carrying off her outfit with ease. She looked as young as her mama and papa, but only I know that age. When the elegant lady spoke she had a soft calming voice that glided across the sound waves like molten chocolate.

'Shamalamaaaaaaamooomooo. Hello Arty Grape, if that is your real name? I haven't been expecting you, I just know who everyone is and I always like to welcome any new guests that find themselves here. My name isn't that important, so I'm not going to bother giving it to you. Are names important? For instance, my name is Rosie, but my real name is Nancy. When I was younger everybody used to call me by my other name, and then one day I was asked to write my given name down and I forgot what it was and, for several moments, *who* I was too. I had to ask myself, *Who am I?* I could tell you more stories but we just don't have the time.' The elegant lady paused and looked up into a space on the white walls around her. It looked like she was thinking, and it also looked like she was just staring into space and thinking of nothing.

Arty Grape took a moment to look around too. She was standing in a white room, there were no items on the walls and nothing on the floors, it was just a white room and its dimensions were unknown, it seemed to never want to end.

'Isn't the person more important than the name, Arty Grape? What's important to me are the qualities that people possess and the qualities that they try to continually acquire. If you didn't possess certain qualities then I doubt we would have ever met, not like this anyhoooooo but in a very different way, one that may have been less pleasant. Let me apologise to you now, I like to speak in riddles. Do you like riddles? Let's have a riddle right now shall we, to break the ice? If the sky is blue and a chair loud, what is the grass? I know that's an easy one but it's my favourite nonetheless. I've always liked the word "nonetheless". Actually I like the word *"juxtaposition"* even more: you really have to think hard before you say it or at least I do. Right my dear, you should be sleeping right now, and remember if you don't sleep you will go quite, quite mad. That's fine by me by the way, going mad that is, because if you've been to the places I've been to, madness soon becomes just another place to visit from time to time. I wouldn't want to stay there, by the way, or buy a holiday home there, just visit it and come back when I've had enough.'

The word *madness* penetrated Arty Grape's thoughts. It went in through her nose and continued its way upwards until it settled in her mind. She began to think about madness, where it is and... *How do you get there*? She had never asked for directions before. That would seem silly, wouldn't it?

'Excuse me sir. Do you know how I can get to madness?'

'I do indeed. Just go down this road and take a left at Nervous Breakdown Street. You can't miss it.'

'Madness I hear you think, my dear. Sometimes madness is right beside you and you wouldn't even know it. I think I went to madness many years ago. Or I might be going next week, I can't remember which. Would you like some Dip Dab? I can't get enough of the stuff.' The elegant lady wandered off and then wandered back again, pacing round and round things that weren't even there, or only she could see. 'My apologies again, dear Arty Grape, I'm purposefully trying to confuse you. What you need to know is that you will meet many people along the way who will try to confuse you, I'm sure you already have, but once you know what they are trying to do it all becomes much more clear. You must look at actions more than you look at the words. These attempts to confuse will continue until we evolve into perfect human beings and we do away with all that kind of silliness, or we go back to the way we were. We've created a perfect place, or at least another world, for ourselves here in Eden. Right now we're just trying to iron out the glitches. Beef jerky?' The elegant lady held out some beef jerky. Arty Grape was hungry so she accepted the generous offer, and it didn't taste as bad as she thought it would.

'Can you be in two places at the same time?' the elegant

lady continued. 'I've been trying to figure that one out for some time now. Listen to me going on! Oh well, you have nowhere else to go do you? You're all mine now.'

Everything was very confusing to Arty Grape, so the elegant lady had accomplished what she had set out to do. She didn't know where she was, she had forgotten how she had got there, and she had no idea who the elegant lady was or what she was saying. 'Sometimes even I wonder if I make sense, but I do, you just have to listen between the lines. Of course you must be wondering who I am, where you are, and what this place is, and possibly how long its been here? It's not a bad place, but to many it may seem that way. What we try to do here is a good thing. When people start experimenting on other people, have we stepped over any boundaries or is it for the greater good? Because that's what we do here, to answer question number five in the reading material you have in your hand. It's all in the book, you should familiarise yourself with it when you have time.'

Arty Grape looked in her hand, and she seemed to be holding a small pamphlet titled 'Indoctramentation'.

'We experiment with people.. people have been doing it for years, but of course that can never be known. How else do you think we find out who and what we are?'

The elegant lady began to walk around the room again and Arty Grape just waited for her to come back. She walked back and forth, side to side, and then she sat down on a red chair that had always been there. Arty Grape was even more confused with what the elegant lady had just said. She accessed the part of her mind that stored the definition of the word 'experiment'. Her papa had always told her to look up words in the dictionary if she didn't know their meaning, just like his papa had told him to do. There was a time when the dictionary had become Arty Grape's favourite book, so she knew what the word meant. She could clearly see the pages in her mind, it was like she had the good book in her hand:

experiment
pronounciation: / Iksperiment(a)nt /
Sperin(a)nt /
1: A scientific procedure undertaken to make a discovery, test, hypothesis, or demonstrate a known fact: 'a laboratory which carried out experiments on pigs'

Even though Arty Grape understood what it meant, she still wondered what kinds of things occurred in this place of hers. She took a moment to look at the white room that she had found herself in: it didn't look as large anymore and she noticed that the walls were now covered in slanted framed pictures of the elegant lady. Every picture was different. The elegant lady was pulling a strange and different face in each of them, some hilarious and others very strange.

'You don't really know where you are do you, Arty Grape? That's okay because nobody else knows where they are, either. They think they do but they have no idea, they just keep pretending, as if it's all normal and everything is okay.' The elegant lady paused and looked up at a blank space on the wall again. 'Mmmmmm. What should we do with you Arty Grape? Where should we take you first? There are so many things in this place of mine and yours to see. Mmmmmm, what to do, what to do?' The elegant lady spun around on the spot. Then she spun some more until she was positively dizzy, stumbling a little after she had finished. 'Aaaaaaah Haaaaa.' She pointed. 'Follow me. I know where we should start. It's really interesting and I think you'll like it.' She turned on her spot like a Shinzan soldier waiting for the next command.

Arty Grape didn't know what to do. As the elegant lady continued to look ahead of and stand as still as she could,

Arty Grape didn't know if she needed to say something or not, so she waited some more.

The elegant lady turned her head towards her without moving the rest of her body. 'You're supposed to tell me you want to follow me,' she whispered through the side of her mouth. 'I can't take you unless you give me permission.'

'Oooooh. Sorry I was wondering if you were waiting for me, I wasn't sure what to do.'

'Never be sure Arty Grape, always be unsure about everything. So... will you follow me, Arty Grape?'

And will you follow me?

Lets Rock

A door opened in a wall of the white room and the elegant lady beckoned Arty Grape to follow her towards it. Arty Grape was drawn to the door and to the elegant lady. She had become enticed by her magic and she would follow her anywhere.

At first she thought it was the door that she had entered through. It *was* the same door, but the room that should have been behind it was now gone, and Arty Grape had walked back into her own bedroom. She saw herself in the bed that she had not long left, sleeping silently, dreaming of all those wonderful thoughts, dreaming about meeting herself in her own dreams; but this wasn't a dream, this was really happening. Her bag was over there and her coat was where it shouldn't have been. *Can you be in two places at the same time?* she asked herself. That question had been asked and now answered, but she still didn't believe it was possible because it had never happened until now.

She watched herself sleep, and then she slowly watched herself wake. Waking up was always a slow process for Arty Grape, she was always desperate to stay in her warm bed and in her warm dreams, not having to face the world that had been randomly put in front of her. Arty Grape watched herself sit up in her bed, and then she swung her feet on to the floor and she saw herself cross the room towards herself. Arty Grape looked at Arty Grape, Arty Grape walked around Arty Grape and then Arty Grape looked herself up and then down. Arty Grape smiled and Arty Grape looked confused, she assumed she must have been dreaming, so she walked back to her bed and laid back down. She pulled the covers over herself and fell asleep almost immediately.

Arty Grape started to feel dizzy and everything started to blur into everything else. Even her thoughts became diluted with other thoughts that she hadn't even had yet, it made her feel nauseous. Something strange was happening to her. She was trapped in a head spin, there was nothing she could do, and her head would spin until it decided to stop. Worlds were colliding, and would continue to collide until her world became one and her state of mind returned.

She found herself in a different room. It was a room that you didn't want to leave. Children of all ages sat with great posture, some small and some very tall. It was a classroom filled with young minds. Each mind was keen and eager to learn everything they could about the world around them and how to live in that world the right way – everything was new to them, everything had just begun. The laws of the universe didn't apply to them yet as they hadn't learned them, so they lived outside every one of its silly laws.

There's one thing about space and time that you should know: when you throw it into a black hole different things start to occur, the rules can be rewritten. I've rewritten some and Arty Grape was about to rewrite hers too.

Arty Grape sat at her usual desk and she looked towards the front of the classroom. She could see the word *thoughtfulness* written on a transparent screen. MissSomeBodyElse was talking to the children, and she placed herself to the side of the words written on the screen.

She didn't sound like she was preaching or teaching, she just talked and asked questions. She even answered some of them herself. Every boy and every girl had the opportunity to answer if they wanted to, and most did. There were no wrong answers, it was a discussion of ideas and thoughts. Everyone was calm and thoughtful to each other but most of all they were attentive whenever MissSomeBodyElse talked.

'A famous philosopher once said, that's right, a famous philosopher. Philosophers are famous in their own world too. That's because they wrote things down, or somebody wrote it down for them and it became translated completely into the wrong thing over many years and centuries. The written word is a powerful thing, even when it's written down incorrectly. It has been a strong force since the day it was invented.' MissSomeBodyElse walked over to her birdcage that was full of books, rummaged around and then pulled out a piece of crumpled paper from one of the books; she looked at it intently then discarded it over her shoulder. 'Remind me at the end children, I mustn't forget about a cake I am baking, I'm having guests for tea. Where were we? In ancient Greece a philosopher called Aristotle became famous for his ideas, but not at the time mind you. He was actually sentenced to death for them, and when asked to renounce his ideas or be executed, he chose to be executed. He was regarded as quite an annoying person. Whether right or wrong, he will be remembered forever. Aristotle introduced the science of happiness. "What is the ultimate purpose of human existence?" he asked, and he argued that happiness is the totality of one's life and not something that could be gained or lost in a few hours. It's how well you have lived, up until this moment, your full potential. Am I happy? This should be the question we ask ourselves consistently. Not only that, but do you believe it when someone tells you they are happy? What does being happy mean, and can you truly

102

be happy? Is happiness a constant of elusiveness, can it ever be reached? Maybe we should ask ourselves why it *may* be impossible to be truly happy? Mmmmmmmm...' MissSomeBodyElse paused, it was like she was formulating her thoughts for the very first time. 'I personally believe that happiness can never be defined or reached. We have some good definitions of happiness, of course, but how can we be certain that those definitions are correct? The earth was once square and the sun once became jealous of the moon.' MissSomeBodyElse giggled to herself like a child, and then she giggled to herself again moments later. She liked a good old giggle, it made her *happy*. 'Let's sit here and think about happiness, but we will need some certainty first. We will base that certainty on Aristotle's definition, because I don't have anything else to mind right now and you can't base anything on uncertainty... apart from uncertainty itself, that is!'

It was the first time Arty Grape had sat in a classroom. Until now she had always been taught by her parents who never wanted her to stray into the outside world, and they only taught her what they wanted her to know. Did you know that the animal world has no interest in human society? They took one look at it and they said, 'No thank you, these human beings are so stupid.'

'I've just remembered something,' said MissSomeBodyElse 'I have the answer on how to be happy, but you're not going to like it. We either have to go back to the past or we have to wait for the future. But anyway, back to happiness...'

Each child was asked to give their opinion and they were allowed to express any thoughts that they had. 'Miss, can I ask another question?' asked one of the taller boys--Of course the boy could ask a question, he was allowed to ask any question he pleased. 'Are we responsible for the happiness of other people?' he said.

'That's a good question Atticus. We all have choices no

matter how hard that choice may be. I believe we are not responsible for the happiness of other people – but if we have taken the choice of happiness away from them, then they are reliant on upon us to make them happy. Isn't that an awful power to abuse? I'm going to take away what happiness you have, I am going to take away your choice!'

Arty Grape thought for a moment, and her eyes rolled into the corner that eyes roll towards when you're thinking instead of lying. She wanted to answer that question. 'Happiness is... Happiness is something you feel inside not outside. If someone is feeling sad then you should be able to give them some of your happiness.'

'Beautiful!' MissSomeBodyElse shouted. 'I love it! I want to ask, what would it feel like to be happy all the time? If you never felt sad then wouldn't happy eventually become sad? Unless I'm looking at it from the wrong direction: happiness as a feeling instead of an actual state? Feelings come and go, but states can sometimes be here to stay. What happens when you reach the state of mind of happiness, can you stay there forever? What is the point of feelings if it's the state of the mind that we want to be in? Do feelings make us human? Wouldn't we just be different types of humans if we didn't have them, and maybe better people? Maybe we can't be happy all the time, it's just the way it's meant to be, and we can't comprehend any other way right now. Just like when the remote control is never where you left it.'

The class murmured to each other for a little while before Luciius put his hand up. He was gestured to speak by MissSomeBodyElse. 'Maybe we can be truly happy, but to be truly happy we have to have the choice of being able to do whatever we want, whenever we want, without it affecting somebody else's happiness. Whatever makes us happy we do, only then can you find it?'

'That's interesting...' MissSomeBodyElse said in a

pondering way. 'But what if it is impossible to do everything you wanted to do, when you wanted to do it? What about death, the ticking clock of inevitable doom? We are born to fail and born to eventually face death, our only friend in the end.' MissSomeBodyElse paced back and forth, the class waited silently and patiently whilst she looked back and forth at her watch. She hummed the words *Mmmmmmmmm* as she walked. 'Okay children, we'll leave it there for now. We need to go back now, back in time that is, to a part of this story that has already happened and is happening right now.

There's No Place Like Home

It was morning in the household, and everything was silent, even the mouse. Mama and Papa weren't sleeping and they weren't trying to spend as much time as they could in their bed. They were upstairs. They were talking to each other and preparing a breakfast for themselves before the children arose. The sun had risen a few hours ago, but the light streaming through the large windows was still perfect, it was warm and golden, illuminating everything with its glow.

'It's strange that Arty and Mr Fox aren't up yet,' said Papa.

'It *is* strange,' said Mama.

'Oooh well. Let's enjoy the peace and quiet for now. I'll check on them in a minute, just to make sure the little ▒▒▒▒ ▒▒▒▒▒▒▒.'

Mama laughed out loud, nearly spitting her milky coffee everywhere. She passed Papa his breakfast. 'There you go my darling, a platter of goodness for you. Are you going to make some juice?' she asked.

'Is it my turn? I'm sure I did it last time? I remember, it was Tuesday, you were still in bed and I brought it down to you. I'm sure I did,' said Papa.

'No you didn't, I did it last time, I remember, it was Wednesday. You fell asleep on the sofa and I brought you juice when you woke up. I remember because you were still fully dressed and you had your headphones on.'

Mama was gaslighting Papa, she did it all the time, but then again we all do it. If you do it purposefully that's a different story, and a question for the sick mind.

Papa said, 'Okay. I'll do it then, but I'm going to remember this.' (No he wasn't.)

Papa ate his breakfast, while mama pottered around the kitchen wandering from cupboard to cupboard in her grey leopard print dressing gown, tidying, wiping and talking. Papa ate his healthy breakfast that consisted of banana, walnuts, avocado, celery and then some humous. He was stuffed by the time he had finished. Nuts are really filling you know? You don't need to eat for hours if you eat nuts, the only problem is they cost a fortune in my time.

Mama eventually sat down and ate her breakfast, she munched and she crunched. They sat in silence and they also talked.

'Should we check on them?' Papa said.

'Do we have to?' Mama asked.

'Not really, I'm sure they're fine. Let's leave it a bit longer. If we hear screams or a body hitting the floor, then we'll check.'

'Deal!' mama said holding out her hand to be shaked.

They sat and talked a little longer around the kitchen table, and then Papa got up and cleared the remaining mess that was left. They sat and waited, and gave themselves twenty minutes more before Papa would check on his children--who weren't there. To him it was mere minutes until the hell would begin. All that he needed was more time: more time to relax, more time to do all the things he wanted to do – but that time had already started to countdown.

'Okay. I'll go down and check on them now,' he said.

'Okay.'

He walked down the stairs as quietly as he could. If they

were asleep, he definitely didn't want to wake them. If he didn't wake them, he could have another five minutes or more. Slowly he stepped down the wooden and creaky staircase. He made his way to ▓ Arty Grape and Mr Fox's bedroom door, and he opened it just enough to fit his head through, he didn't want to be seen or heard. He peered through the tiny gap – and he wasn't startled by the empty beds that he discovered. Arty Grape and Mr Fox weren't there, so he closed the door quietly again and he calmly walked back upstairs and sat back down. 'They're not there,'

'They're not there,' replied Mama.

They both looked at each other and they smiled like Cheshire cats. Their dream of not having children had come true – or their dream of somebody taking their children had, either way they were smiling about the delightful situation they found themselves in.

'It's about time, I was wondering when they would leave, or should I say, be taken.'

Here enters the NoWhereMan, he appears from time to time as I told you he would. He is the watcher of worlds, interfering only when necessary. It wasn't necessary here, so he decided to interfere. 'Hello Mama, hello Papa?' said the NoWhereMan. The NoWhereMan was sitting in the living room on their blue suede sofa. Mama and Papa couldn't see him but they had heard him. They walked into the living room to see who was talking to them, and there he sat, unnoticed. 'Hello Mama and Papa.'

'Hello,' they both said in unison.

They sat down, and then he stood up. They were playing a game of musical chairs, but it was his game not theirs. He looked them both carefully in the eyes and then he left.

Before the NoWhereMan had arrived they didn't care about the disappearance of their beautiful children, but upon his exit they had buried it so deep down that they didn't even remember they had children. It was seven years before the children were returned and when they returned it was like they had never left.

If it's okay I'd like to share a little secret with you? I cannot tell you who the NoWhereMan is, not even I know, he has become such a part of me that I'm not sure who is who anymore. If I discover who he is I'll be sure to let you know in the pages of this ever growing book.

Arty Grape and Mr Fox were no longer in the house, so it was time for the NoWhereMan to leave too. The only reason he was in the town of Eden was to follow their journey and find out who they would eventually become. He had to find them and maybe help them, if they needed to be helped. The NoWhereMan knew Arty Grape and Mr Fox wouldn't be too far away or to far in in front of him He knew they needed to struggle through the forest first, he knew Mr Fox had to come close to death, he knew they had to meet the strange little girl with the strange haircut. He knew there was a lot more that they had to discover.

The NoWhereMan knew all the short cuts through the forest to the tower on the hill, he had after all been there many times before, he had always been a welcomed guest, just like Arty Grape and Mr Fox would soon find themselves to be. He worked his way across the town and into the forest that surrounded it. He walked through the trees, he crossed the river and he climbed the mountain. It wasn't long before he spotted them lost amongst the trees. He hadn't noticed them at first, but as soon as he did he began to move quietly. If only he hadn't stepped on that large, yet weak branch. The sound of a it snapping echoed through the forest and Arty Grape and Mr Fox immediately turned to look. The trees were too thick and the light still too dim for them to see the NoWhereMan. He blended himself into the forest, he didn't want to be seen, not just yet anyway. He looked at them and he thought to himself how tired they had become and he hoped that they would get to their very end.

Arty Grape and Mr Fox turned around and continued their journey and the NoWhereMan continued his. He carried on climbing, enjoying the colours of the forest, he basked in the light slowly edging its way towards him. He was back to nature, he was roaming free again and he didn't need anything else, he just needed to be part of the forest again, it was where he had been born. He walked, and he listened to the sounds the forest had to offer whilst carefully navigating his way. Even though he knew the forest like the back of his hand, he knew he had to respect it, he knew he could stumble if he wasn't concentrating. The trees spoke to him in their own language, the water sang as it meandered down the river, he was in his very own heaven, he had been to heaven, yet he still loved the forest more. He walked and he walked and he then thought to himself *it's time to take a rest now*. The NoWhereMan found a quiet spot in the corner of the forest. He stood still and he took the time to breathe. He needed a moment to himself to process his thoughts. He had let them build up and he needed to put some of them in the recycle bin. He took down his hood and unzipped his coat, and then he felt even more free – free from the shackles he had given himself in this world. He breathed deeply and inhaled the fresh morning air, and he listened to the birds sing. He too could still hear the sound of the water even though it wasn't there anymore. It suddenly dawned on him: he was late. If he was going to get to where he needed to be, he would have to run, so that's what he did. He bolted into the forest as fast as you can imagine, and he didn't stop. He jumped over fallen trees, avoiding the brambles in his way. He didn't stop for any fool. Arty Grape would see him later. They would always find him in the most unlikely of places.

Lets Rock

We're back now. I hope you enjoyed my little detour? I'll try to keep the story flowing in the right direction. Now, where were we? I think Arty Grape was sat at her desk and MissSomeBodyElse was talking to the class about happiness. Shall we continue....

Arty Grape was anxious about the bell ringing and then she became anxious about whether a bell actually existed. She wanted to stay in the room she was in, she wanted to listen more, learn more, but there isn't enough time in the whole world to learn everything, even the universe is running out of time. Arty Grape was afraid it was going to end too soon and the feeling of elation would would leave her forever.

MissSomeBody entered the room but really it was MissSomeBodyElse pretending to be MissSomeBody. She had only added a pair of glasses to her costume, it wasn't much of a disguise. She walked over to herself and whispered in her own ear before turning to the class. 'Arty Grape can you come with me please & thank you?'

'Arty Grape off you go please,' said MissSomeBodyElse.

Arty Grape opened her wooden desk and gathered up all her things, her fluffy pencil case and her trusty pen. She popped them in her bag, put on her cardigan and trotted out of the room and into the corridor and waited for

MissSomeBody.

'I just wanted to have a quick chat with you to see how you're getting on. You've been here for fifteen weeks now and from what we can see, because we are watching you, you're fitting in very nicely, as I knew you would. How do you feel Arty Grape? Feelings are important, just as much as thoughts. Being trapped in your mind is never a good thing, but feelings combined with the thoughts, now there's a different thing completely. How are you feeling Arty Grape and *how* are *you* feeling? What has been the best part of your day today? It's a question that's often overlooked; nevertheless it is an important question to ask others and to ask yourself.'

Confused thoughts flooded into Arty Grape's head. She remembered having had them not long ago and having the same feeling. She didn't remember how she had got there or if she had been there for six weeks, two weeks or ten years? It was all an elusive jumble of things. Arty Grape only knew what she had been told, and she had been told that she had been there for twenty two weeks.

She stood at MissSomeBody's side and walked down the corridors, moving from one corridor to another. Slowly she was being hypnotised by MissSomeBody and by each of the rooms she had visited along the way. *How long have I been here now?* she thought. It really didn't matter anymore and she didn't care. Every moment lived was gone, and the memory of each slowly faded as time passed. Arty Grape belonged here now and she was absorbing as much as she could from the tower. Soon it would all be over, and she would find herself back in her bed again, her warm lovely bed that she never really left. Arty Grape continued to drift down corridors that had started to look the same. Only by looking at the words written on the many doors in her mind did she know it was a different corridor, with different things to explore.

MissSomeBody kept talking as they walked; she never stopped, even when Arty Grape stopped to gaze at some of the doors she would continue to ramble. It didn't matter to her if another soul was listening. 'Come along Arty Grape,' she would call out at different intervals along the way, and Arty Grape would hurry back to her side. 'Come along Arty Grape,' she would call again.

Arty Grape turned to follow MissSomeBody, and as she turned she found herself sitting in a new room and in a new chair, she was as confused as you are right now. Sitting next to her was the NoWhereMan, he was talking and gesticulating at somebody in front of him. She sat and listened to him speak but she couldn't understand him, he spoke in a different language and he spoke that language back to front.

With a blink of your fingers and the snapping of an eye, everything changed once again. Sitting directly in front of her were three men wearing the same suits in the same shade of grey, looking equally as bored as each other. They were the grey men and they looked incredibly formal. They wore grey suits and they wore a sad, stern look on their grey faces. They had grey shoes, grey bowties and grey bowler hats. The grey men were defending the space between themselves with a solid looking table. The three men stared at Arty Grape for a second, or five, you could see that they were all thinking of what to say, and they were all thinking about who was going to be the first person to say something. Would it be me, would it be they, or would it be them? One of the grey men started to look Arty Grape up and down, and once he had finished looking her up and down, the other grey man began to do the same. The three grey men opened up their notepads. It didn't feel like a very fun place to be for Arty Grape. They repeatedly fired questions at her, all at the same time.

'Why are you here?'
'Where did you come from?'
'What do you think you want?'
'Where do you think you are going?'
'When are we?'
'What are we?'
'There's no place like home.'
'There is no place.'

Everything became white noise to Arty Grape, each of their words dissolving into the next one.

One by one they stopped talking, until only one of the grey men spoke. 'We've just met your wonderful brother Mr Fox. He asked about you, of course he did. "Never mind," he said. "I'm sure I'll see her after." I remember thinking that it was a strange way to end a sentence--*after*. After *what?* I thought. Arty Grape? Did you hear me?'

When Arty Grape looked up the strange grey men didn't seem strange to her anymore. The stern appearances on their faces, and their grey look, had vanished. Their faces were alight with smiles and they weren't wearing suits anymore. The grey men were looking very cool and very casual.

'Mr Fox!' Arty Grape shouted out with delight. Truth be told, Mr Fox was somebody else's memory to Arty Grape, she had forgotten who she was, and who he was up until this very moment.

'How could we forsake you Arty Grape? How lucky it is that you found us on your own. By my records we should have met you many years ago. On behalf of us all I apologise. It's never happened before. Make a note, it mustn't happen again,' said one of the grey men.

One of the other grey men started flicking though some papers on his desk and he wrote something down on his notepad; then everything was silent for a few moments.

'We have many classes here Arty Grape. Of course we have

the usual things, but what we like to concentrate on are the important things. The Yin shall we say. Let's just say you are an exceptional young lady and, even though you've arrived later than you should have, we can place you exactly where you're supposed to be. You will learn many things here Arty Grape, and we hope that they will stay with you forever, even though you won't remember them, they will still be there for you to discover at another time of readiness. Qualities that you wish to see in others, you too will also have.'

'We just wanted to meet you Arty Grape and say *Godspeed.'* said another one of the men.

'Yes, Arty Grape. Godspeed, no harm will come to you here, or at least I don't think it will.'

MissSomeBody entered the room. She looked at Arty Grape and looked at each of the men behind the table. 'Sorry to bother you. May I take Arty Grape now or do you want to talk a little more?'

'Of course MissSomeBody, you are most welcome to her. I imagine she is very keen to continue her journey through the tower, and maybe she has already begun to question where she came from and how she got here. It will do you no good Arty Grape, thinking all the time. It will stop you sleeping, it will drive you insane. Will I see you later or should I say after?' he smiled.

'Let's Rock!' danced MissSomeBody. She snapped her fingers and then flashed her hands in front of Arty Grape's eyes and she found herself surrounded by her emptiness once more.

Irreducible Complexity

Irreducible Complexity. Isn't that a fancy phrase? It turns out it's not that fancy after all.

For a long time Arty Grape found herself alone, she hoped somebody would come for her and take her back to the land of the living – what had she done to deserve this? She became scared that her journey was over and this was her final resting place, floating in the dark emptiness that surrounded her, she felt like she was blindfolded in a sensory deprivation tank.

Time kept passing her by and still nobody came for her, she was all alone. She remained hopeful but that hope was slowly dwindling. Poor Arty Grape, she had gone through so much. Maybe she had opened the wrong door? Maybe she had made the wrong choice along the way? She didn't know what was to become of her. Maybe Mr Fox would arrive to save her sometime soon? Maybe her mama or papa would be shaking her awake, and any moment now she would find herself back in her beautiful bed? *But somebody is already in my bed,* she thought.

Was she still Arty Grape or had she been replaced? She was still on the rollercoaster, and she didn't realise she was on a rollercoaster until she was half way around the loop-deloop.

'There you are Arty Grape. How did you end up here?' said a voice. She could hear MissSomeBody, but she couldn't see her. 'We've been looking for you. You wandered off. You mustn't wander off, these doors and these corridors need someone who knows how to navigate them. You can walk in one room and you can find yourself coming out the next. Stay with me, we're nearly finished. We'll release you soon enough, then you can go back to your beautiful bed, that's what you were thinking about wasn't it?' MissSomeBody stared long and hard at Arty Grape. 'I'll let you decide where we go next my dear.'

Arty Grape saw MissSomeBody appear in front of her, she thought she had imagined her silhouette standing in the door frame, but she was really there. MisSomeBody beckoned Arty Grape to follow her once again.

'Tell me, where do you want to go? Your wish is my command. Follow me Arty Grape and keep thinking about what room you want to visit next.'

MissSomeBody held out her hand and guided her off. They walked once again along the maze of corridors. Arty Grape knew which door she wanted to find, she knew it was down some corridor somewhere, all she had to do was think about it and it would appear before her.

'Aaaah. Arty Grape, I know where that room is, just follow me and I'll take you there.' said MissSomeBody. She began to walk faster; she had more excitement in her step than before. 'Come. Keep up, we'll be there soon, it's just around another three corners.'

Arty Grape walked as fast as she could to keep up with MissSomeBody and at times she stumbled and fell, but no matter what she always stayed by the side of her teacher until she reached her final destination.

MissSomeBody suddenly came to a skip and a jump before

she stopped and clapped her hands together. 'Here we are,' she said. Arty Grape had been brought to the exact door that she had been thinking of, but had never said aloud. It was a door made entirely of mottled glass and the word *love* was beautifully written on its surface. Arty Grape reached for the glass doorknob, turned it and opened the door to find Miss MissSomeBodyElse standing in the room. She turned to Arty Grape and welcomed her in, she wanted to see what condition her condition was in.

'Hello, Arty Grape, it's nice to see you again. I hope MissSomeBody has been looking after you. Come join us, we've kept your usual seat for you.'

Arty Grape walked into the room. It seemed like she had been there before, but there were different children and they were discussing a different topic, and also the room was completely different too--I take that last sentence back, she didn't feel like she had been there before.

The children in the room were discussing the topic of love. As a young girl I never discussed love in any of the classrooms I sat in. Have you? Maybe that should be part of the curricalumulem-aaaahhh.

Arty Grape sat in her usual seat and she couldn't help smiling on the inside and on the out. She was happy, and all the other children seemed to be experiencing pure happiness too. MissSomeBodyElse talked and talked and she passed on her definition of love and she added the children's thoughts in to the mix--Children question everything! What a pain in the beep ba beep beep beep they can be. Question everything Arty Grape once told me, leave no stone unturned.

MissSomeBodyElse stopped talking and spun around to look at the clock behind the side of her. 'So. We've spent the last hour talking about love. Now what I want you to do is go away and think more carefully about it. Examine it, analyse it, figure out what it means to you. Question whether it means the same thing to all of us, and if it doesn't, then why not? People love others so much they end up doing terrible things to them, its as if they was to possess and then consume them. Think about that. We'll talk more next time, we have a lot more thinking to do.'

It was time to leave the room so the children began to gather up their things, Arty Grape did what she usually did at the end of each class and packed up all her pencils and all her pens before tidying them into her backpack, then she followed the other children.

Just as she was about to leave MissSomeBodyElse called to her, 'Not you Arty Grape, you wait here for a minute, I'd like to talk to you.'

'Okay.' she said.

'Just give me a few moments, I'll be right with you.' MissSomeBodyElse began to tidy her desk, opening and closing drawers, putting things away and then pulling things out and putting them in places they shouldn't be. At one point she pulled out a sandwich and took a bite out of it before putting it in one of her pockets. 'Shall we go?' she said, but it wasn't really a question. 'There is one last thing I want to show you. It's an important room that we sometimes overlook.

Welcome To

Arty Grape followed MissSomeBodyElse out of the room. They drifted past many doors, they turned left, then right, and then they went up some stairs and then back down the same stairs. They passed several children as they walked, each of them flashing Arty Grape a wonderful smile, to signal their friendliness.

'What a good little girl you are Arty Grape. Obeying my every command. We've conditioned you correctly I see. Well, we're here.' MissSomeBodyElse stood in front of a door, deliberately hiding the words that were written on it. She stood and looked at Arty Grape briefly, before swiftly slipping to one side, allowing Arty Grape to stare at the place where the words were usually written... but she couldn't see anything, no words, letters, riddles or rhymes.

Arty Grape was more curious than ever as to what she would find over the next threshold. Arty Grape started to put one foot in front of the other, and MissSomebodyElse slowly opened the door. Very slowly and very carefully Arty Grape worked her way inside, MissSomeBodyElse slowly closed the door behind Arty Grape, without joining her. She stood in the middle of the room and looked around to discover the it was beautifully decorated. It was the most colourful room she had ever been in: painted artwork adorned its walls, sculpted pieces were dotted across any surface they could find, and written word vandalised the walls.

Arty Grape became drawn to everything she saw. Once she had finished digesting one part of the room, she would digest another. She had become so lost in the beauty and warmth of the room that she hadn't even noticed Mr Fox sitting at the very back of it. He had blended quite nicely into the colourful walls. He didn't want to interrupt his sister, he knew exactly what she was thinking and feeling because only moments ago he had felt the same. 'Mr Fox! Where did you come from? I didn't see you there,' she shouted as she ran towards him. Mr Fox shot up and ran towards her too and they collided into each other and held each other tight before bursting into tears. 'I had forgotten about you. I'm sorry, I'm so sorry. I love you,' she blubbered.

'I love you too.'

'I don't know who I am anymore. I'm lost but I don't want to leave,' she said. 'Where are we now, do you know? What room are we in? Where will we go next? Will we see each other again?'

Mr Fox didn't answer his sister. He didn't know what was next, he never thought to ask, he just followed his nose and his nose followed him. They felt like they had reached their final destination in the tower on the hill, they had reached it together. That was all that mattered to them now.

'Where has MissSomeBodyElse gone?' asked Mr Fox

'I don't know, she closed the door but she didn't come in.'

'Maybe she's still outside.'

A voice shouted from the far side of the room, 'Yooohooooo, I'm over here.' MissSomeBodyElse was warming her hands by the stove of fire that was burning in the corner. 'I bet you two thought you'd never see me again didn't you? Sorry about that, I had to pop to the loo.' MissSomeBodyElse turned around and began warming her butt, wiggling it from side to side, evenly spreading the heat. 'Aaaah. There's nothing like a good butt warming.'

'I'll wager that you thought I didn't even exist,' said MissSomeBody standing behind them.

'Don't worry. We get that all the time.' said MissSomeBodyElse

'Don't forget to remember all the things you've learned here. Our hope is that they've become a part of you now and a part of everyone else too,' said MissSomeBody. 'You've been here seven years and its time you were leaving. We didn't have enough time to talk about everything, but we think we've shown you the most important things.'

It was the last time that they saw MissSomeBody and MissSomeBodyElse. The elegant ladies joined each other at the front of the room, smiled and clicked their fingers, and then they were gone. They weren't coming back but they would never be forgotten.

On the wall behind them some words had been written for Arty Grape and Mr Fox, they walked closer so they could see them. The words said *Welcome To Death*, and as soon as they had finished reading them the walls around them began to turn. They turned until they began to spin. It was like they were trapped inside a zoetrope that never wanted to stop doing what it was designed to do. The room span, and they spun, the world around them slowly absorbed into itself; it melted right in front of Arty Grape's eyes, it was grotesque to look at and it disturbed her senses. People and places began to evaporate, babies were born and then silenced. Her brother slowly began to melt away in front of her eyes. Arty Grape felt like she was standing inside a raging fire that burnt her being down to her very soul. There was no end to the torment that Arty Grape felt – she only hoped that it would be over soon and she would be free of all the pain it brought. Finally, a serene silence fell over her; but it wasn't silence, it was acceptance of her inevitable fate.

No one knows whether death, which people fear to be the greatest evil, may be the greatest good.

Time Ran Away

Mr Fox and Arty Grape found each other again in that place you find yourself in sometimes. It was a peculiar place – peculiar because they had been there before. They emerged on a spot that they'd stood in before, not just in the same spot but the same time too; they had been in this time before. The strange man with the strange eyes stood in front of them, he looked at them like he had done the very first time they'd met him. 'Welcome. You are most welcome,' he said.

Arty Grape couldn't move, she had absolutely no control over what was happening, what had happened or what was going to happen. *Time* had brought them back to this place and *Time's* tricks didn't end there either. Arty Grape stood holding her brothers hand, peering once again into the black void of the entrance to the tower on the hill and the entrance gazed back at them. *It would be rude not to go in,* she thought. But they didn't go in, instead she wondered about everything that had come before this moment, all the things they had learned in each and every one of the rooms that the tower had to offer. Arty Grape didn't know what was real any more, she didn't know who was telling what truths, when everyone lies to you, there is no place to find the truth, there is no where to turn to until the tower finds you.

The personality of *Time* started to show a different side of itself, a side that Arty Grape had never seen before: *Time* stopped and it then it started to reverse.

Arty Grape and Mr Fox began to move backwards, without turning around. With every backward step everything in front of them slowly drifted away, every moment, every second and every feeling. Their whole world and its existence was being sucked away. Every recorded memory was being taken, stolen from their minds. They journeyed backwards through their own time and they became one with the universe. They knew that feeling wouldn't last, it rarely does. Travelling backwards in time they went: physically, metaphorically, and even actually. On their backwards journey they tried to understand the mistakes that were made, but it was too late – that time had already happened and future mistakes had already been made.

The beautiful morning arrived once again in the house and the light pushed itself through any crack that it could find. Its warmth gently caressed Arty Grape's body. She was back in her beautiful bed. It was a slow and peaceful awakening to her new world, her eyes slowly opened and she perused the room and her mind, struggling to reach any kind of conclusion. She had arrived at a new dawn. She was alive and the sun was shining, what came before didn't matter to her. But it did matter to her. Arty Grape liked to question herself. *Is this really happening? Am I really here?* How could she know if it was just a dream that was as real as you and me? Nothing could erase the thoughts that the tower allowed her to hold on to, the good ones, the bad ones and the ugly ones. These thoughts and feelings would be passed on like a beautiful virus, spreading itself everywhere until there was no place they hadn't infected.

The waves of Beethoven's Symphony No 5 echoed down

the stairs. A delicious smell wandered from the kitchen. *It must be Sunday,* she thought, which always meant popcorn and sweets. She rolled over and reached for her cube shaped clock to discover it was 2:22pm. She climbed out of her bed and searched for her dressing gown. It wasn't cold but she longed for a comfortable memory that would bring good thoughts.

Arty Grape slowly walked upstairs, and the music became louder the further she climbed. She walked through the empty kitchen and into the living room, and there sat Mr Fox on the sofa, waiting for his sister. He looked at her and she at him. Instantly everything became as normal as it once was.

'Hello,' Papa sang.
'Morning Pap,' she replied without even looking at him.

'Today's movie is *Back to the Future,* one of my favourite movies, an old and amazing classic. We have popcorn, we have sweets and we have a dash of the fizzy stuff. Whaddya say to that?'
'Okay,' Arty Grape mumbled, completely unimpressed.
'Okay! Okay! I thought you'd be more excited than that.'
Arty Grape shifted her body to the sofa and sat down next to Mr Fox. He immediately put his arm around her for a cuddle. Seven years had passed without them knowing, but everything had remained the same party from who *they* were, the tower on the hill had altered them without their knowledge.
'Okay you two, a late breakfast, come and sit down,' shouted Papa from the kitchen.
They ran towards the table. They were excited by their breakfast today, it was pancakes with lemon and butter. Papa didn't have to ask them twice to come to the table like he usually did.

They sat and devoured their food, talking like they usually, did but Arty Grape's mind was still in two places – one mind had been left behind in the tower of the hill and the other mind was wondering where the rest of itself had gone. *Am I still here?* she asked herself. She looked down at the table, and the pattern on the tablecloth slowly started to rise up. It slowly worked its way up her body like liquid velvet, it engulfed her bit by bit, it was trying to eat her face and it wasn't going to stop until it had consumed her.

'Arty! Arty! Arty!' someone shouted.

Arty Grape didn't answer.

'Arty Grape!' shouted Papa.

Arty Grape returned to her current reality with a jolt. 'I thought we'd lost you then, Arty. You were away with the fairies, daydreaming again I suppose. What were you thinking of?'

But Arty Grape couldn't remember what she was thinking of. She would often forget, so today was like no different day. She peered over her papa's shoulders and there, over by the kitchen drawers, stood the NoWhereMan. Only Arty Grape seemed to see him; was he another figment of her imagination, like the tower on the hill had been? The NoWhereMan began to dance in circles, slowly spinning around. He spun on the spot but he never became dizzy. The NoWhereMan danced to his own rhythm, it was a beat that Arty Grape was oblivious to; she wished she knew the music that he was listening to in his head, so she could dance with him too. There was something different about the NoWhereMan, and it took her a moment to figure out just what that was: Arty Grape could see his beautiful face! It was a face that could light up a thousand rooms. She recognised him, she had seen his face many times before. He danced and he danced and he smiled and he smiled, looking directly at her with each revolution. His smiled seemed bigger with every turn.

Its time to leave this story now and soon it will be time to fly from these pages. Let's follow the NoWhereMan now, shall we? He will lead us to the very end.

Tomorrow Never Comes

So you made it to the end, the final chapter. I can't believe you made it all the way through this madness, because it is complete madness, and I've often wondered if I've gone mad. Am I going mad or will I end up mad? Have you ever wondered that?

The NoWhereMan danced his way out of the room in a backwards fashion, then he spun around one final time, and paused and pointed at Arty Grape, before taking a courteous bow and walking backwards out of the room. The NoWhereMan always did like a good bow. Just before he disappeared from sight, he said something even Arty Grape didn't hear and just like that, he was gone. He may return to the town of Eden as the NoWhereMan again or he might decide to be someone else. Either way, it was time for the NoWhereMan to go home – he had been gone too long and he had people that he wanted to see, waiting for him. The NoWhereMan's family knew that he liked to drift, but out of respect for those he loved, he didn't drift for too long anymore. Just as Arty Grape and Mr Fox had their journey, he was on his own journey through the world, so he headed home to where it always began.

The NoWhereMan began his walk to the to the train station that never welcomed any trains. It was his only way out of the town of Eden. As he walked he would stop every now and again to figure out where he was, and in which direction he should travel. He knew there would be a train arriving not long after he did, so he couldn't foolishly walk in the wrong direction. He floated through the glorious town of Eden. He had always enjoyed being in Eden when he visited, but he could never stay. To stay in the town of Eden would mean giving up, it would mean he would never see all the other places that were meant to be seen.

People were going about their business in the usual manner, most people that he passed smiled or said hello. The pavements glowed like they had been placed there just for him to walk on. He sauntered around every corner without a care in the world. Nobody knew who he was and he didn't tell them; he was unrecognisable because they could see his face. He passed the beautiful rose gardens, and he inhaled the scent of freshly baked bread in the air. He was delighted by the sound of the children laughing in the playground – it was a joyous sound to hear. It was like the sound of hearing a baby giggle for the first time, amplified one hundred and fifty-one thousand times. He passed many more people on his way, but the closer he walked towards the station, the fewer people he saw. Nobody had reason to visit the train station any more.

He walked up the small incline in the path and through the entrance of the station. He slowly walked down towards the platform, and everything was exactly as he had planned. It was two minutes until the next train to *outta here*. The NoWhereMan could see the train approaching in the distance; he could see half a mile of the track when he stood in the right place. He wondered where the train had come from and where it would take him.

The rickety train ventured slowly into the station, it didn't seem to be in a rush to get anywhere. It pulled up to the edge of the platform, came to a slow halt and made the sound that trains usually make. It sat motionless for a moment, before one of the doors of the many carriages opened. It wasn't the door right in front of him, it was five doors to the left. The door opened, and it stayed open, waiting for a traveller to enter or to leave. The NoWhereMan waited too, he waited for the door to close. *Time* wasn't about to hang around in any station, *Time* needed to keep flowing. The train started to move forwards again, it began to gain speed, it began to whizz past him. All of its colours blended into each other, it pounded on the tracks like it didn't matter, it sped towards its next destination.

The NoWhereMan was still standing on the platform, he hadn't wanted to go to where the train would take him. He glanced around himself, he was checking if there were any other people around, but he knew there wouldn't be. There were no other people that he could see, so he knew it was safe to make his next move. The NoWhereMan reached out in front of himself with one hand and he carefully pulled the curtain of this reality to one side. He paused and then he stepped into the cosmic crack that lay between his world and Arty Grape's. He was going back to where he belonged; no matter how much he liked all the other worlds, he liked his own world best. It was a place that was all the better for having Arty Grape and Mr Fox in it. The NoWhereMan took a large step into his world and then the gap in reality closed behind him. He was plunged into darkness. He knew he had to keep walking, he knew that very soon he would walk back into his own reality of things.

Finally, after several steps, his world appeared to him again. Everything around him glowed with colour, wild animals roamed free and untamed. There were some that could understand animals and others that couldn't. Only if you lived in this world would it appear normal to you – if you didn't, then *it* didn't. It was like living in Limbuckfoo, or south of one of this places. In those places strange things were afoot everywhere you turned, but to the NoWhereMan everything was how it should have been. He wandered through his own world. He stopped to talk to strangers along his way, and he shared whatever food he had if they were hungry. His journey wasn't over yet. In fact, just like Arty Grape's and Mr Fox's had only just begun, so too had the NoWhereMan's.

On his journey home he prospered and he enjoyed life. The world sang to him on many different occasions and, when it did, he liked the tune that it hummed. Lightness and darkness arrived and left, multiple amounts of times. He climbed high mountains, the peaks of some dusted with pure snow. The air was clean, cold and fresh, and with every breath it felt like his body was growing younger. There was no stopping the NoWhereMan getting to where he wanted to go. He was going to the promised land, or at least his own version of the promised land. It was just around the corner, over there or behind that chair. It's always behind that chair. His world didn't look like anything you've read about before in any other book.

His destination was a little house – a house where he would rest his weary travelling head for a little while – but before placing his head on his delicious pillow, he wanted to see the people that were most important to him. His resting place wasn't far away, he could see his humble home and he could see his wonderful partner and beautiful children waiting for him.

Artemis and Lucian Fox ran towards him as he walked down the path to the house. They were excited to see him. Lucian jamp up onto him and forced him backwards. His children had been on a journey too, and they couldn't wait to tell him about it. They both talked at him at exactly the same time, and then they took turns to tell him all about a town called Eden that was not too far away from where they lived.

Whilst he had been gone, Arty and Lucian Fox had busied themselves creating a story. They had conjured characters called Arty Grape and Mr Fox and these imaginary friends had been on an adventure through their minds. They were desperate to read him the first chapter that they had dreamed up, and he couldn't wait to hear it either. They all sat down and the storytelling began.

She woke up the next day. It felt like it usually did, but it wasn't. There was something different but she didn't know what it was or where that feeling had come from. She was experiencing disturbing thoughts and uncomfortable feelings at regular intervals.

It was a school day and she did what she usually did at that time in the morning, which was limiting the chaos that was about to occur.

It's Happening Again.

Thanks

If you've reached this page then I would like to thank you for reading to the end. I hope you liked it.

I would love you to leave a review on Amazon, only if you liked it, remember, if you have nothing good to say then say nothing. I have two more books I will be publishing soon, if you would like to know more about them please leave your details on the contact page of my website.

Arty Grape & The Homework Factory
   Arty Grape & The Devil Inside

Thank you.
   Darius Z. Sutherland

http://artygrape.com/contact.html

References

Come with me and you'll see into a world of pure imagination, we'll begin with a spin into your imagination.Pure Imagination - **Charlie & The Chocolate Factory**

Life is so short, questionable and evanescent that it is not worth the trouble of major effort - **Arthur Schopenhauer.**

Life without pain has no meaning - **Arthur Schopenhauer.**

No man knows whether death, which people fear to be the greatest evil, may not be the greatest good. - **Plato**

Printed in Great
Britain
by Amazon

31253321R10079